The Lambs Lane Affair

Sherlock Holmes Uncovered

Steven Ehrman

DEDICATION

To my father.

DEDICATION III

WORKS BY THE SAME AUTHOR...........................I

CHAPTER ONE 1

CHAPTER TWO 11

CHAPTER THREE..23

CHAPTER FOUR..33

CHAPTER FIVE..45

CHAPTER SIX 57

CHAPTER SEVEN..69

CHAPTER EIGHT 81

CHAPTER NINE 91

CHAPTER TEN..104

CHAPTER ELEVEN 115

CHAPTER TWELVE..**126**

CHAPTER THIRTEEN...**138**

CHAPTER FOURTEEN **150**

CHAPTER FIFTEEN..**161**

CHAPTER SIXTEEN **167**

CHAPTER SEVENTEEN **179**

Steven Ehrman

WORKS BY THE SAME AUTHOR

The Sherlock Holmes Uncovered Tales
The Eccentric Painter
The Iron Dog
The Mad Judge
The Spider Web
The Lambs Lane Affair
The Rising Minister
Coming soon – Robin Hood's Revenge

The Frank Randall Mysteries
The Referral Game
The Visible Suspect

The Zombie Civilization Saga
Zombie Civilization: Genesis
Zombie Civilization: Exodus

CHAPTER ONE

I found myself growing somewhat ill at ease as I sat in the rooms I shared with Sherlock Holmes at 221B Baker Street. Holmes, while never the most convivial of men, had been particularly moody and could not be drawn into conversation. I was used to the taciturn nature of the great detective, but he had become positively surly over the past week.

As I was reading a collection of the poems of Lord Byron, I was startled by my friend slapping the arm of his chair in frustration. I was never an aficionado of the Romantic era poets and was glad for the distraction. Holmes looked up at me and wryly smiled.

"I apologize, Doctor, for disturbing you," said he. "But I know for a fact that you only read Byron when you are recalling the Newfoundland hound of your youth."

I willingly put down the volume to reply.

"So the new day finds you in a communicative mood, Holmes?" I asked. "It has been some few days since I have received a civil reply to any greeting."

"And again, I apologize. This Masterson counterfeiting case has me thoroughly flummoxed. He is a clever man I will grant you, but I will corner him yet."

I was always somewhat surprised whenever Holmes confessed to being out of his depths. In our association he had solved so many cunning mysteries that I thought him incapable of failure, yet I knew in my heart this was not true.

"Perhaps, Holmes," I essayed, "I could be of some aid to you in this matter. Besides the bare necessities, I know nothing of the case, but I have some slight experience in detection, as you know."

Holmes was lighting a pipe as I spoke, and he was soon billowing smoke into the air. It was fortunate that it was a temperate month, as otherwise our lodgings could become quite poisonous from the pungent tobacco Holmes employed.

"I have considered that, Doctor," he said in a contemplative manner. "But I am afraid that the details of the case are quite above your station, and you would be of little use."

I was well acquainted with Holmes's lack of social skills, but even I was taken aback by his brutal comment. If it was true that I did not possess the mind of the great detective, I had aided him materially many times. My dismay must have plainly showed across my face as Holmes quickly moved to soften the blow.

"It is not my intent to demean your intelligence, old friend; it is simply that the case is quite technical, and the effort it would take to acquaint you with the facts would not be worth the effort. What is needed is someone to whom facts and figures are second nature. Such a person might indeed be of aid."

"Why, Holmes," said I. "You have drawn a portrait of someone that you know well. Can you not see the solution? Whom have you just described?"

I saw a trace of concentration cross his brow and his face soon broadened into a smile.

"Why, Watson, as soon as I declare that you cannot help me in this matter, you demonstrate the common sense that does you credit."

Praise was not often coming from Holmes and I allowed myself to bask, for a moment, in the knowledge that I had laid out a solution to his problem that had vexed him for the past week.

"Well, Holmes, a glance at the clock shows that it is nearly five," I said. "Our quarry is safely ensconced in his den by now, if history is any guideline, so perhaps we should be off."

Holmes arose from his chair and clapped me on the shoulder in a gesture of camaraderie. We were soon down the seventeen steps of our home, and after a quick word to Mrs. Hudson, we found ourselves on Baker Street.

The solution that had been obvious to me, and obvious to Holmes as well once broached, was that we should lay the vexing counterfeit problem at the feet of the brother of my friend, Mycroft.

I had been unaware of the existence of any family members that Holmes had before the affair of the Greek Interpreter. It had been vaguely in my head that since Holmes was reticent in the extreme about discussing his antecedents, he simply did not have any. I was greatly surprised at his bland description of a brother who lived a scant few miles away in Pall Mall.

This brother, Mycroft Holmes, was a man of most eccentric habits, even for a close relation of Sherlock Holmes. Holmes had vaguely told me that Mycroft was employed by the government in a position of auditing the books of various departments. He seemed unwilling to go into the matter any deeper and I was loath to pursue it further in the face of his disinclination.

Mycroft belonged to, and indeed helped found, one of the most singular clubs in all of London. The Diogenes Club was located near Mycroft's rooms in Pall Mall and was an association of the most non-congenial men in existence. Conversation was forbidden in the club, save for the Stranger's Room, and any man who was so incommodious to his fellow members as to break this code three times became a former member at once.

To all observance the club seemed to be no different than any other club of like-minded men in the city. It was filled with comfortable armchairs, cheery fireplaces, and the papers and periodicals of the day.

Holmes's brother was a patron of the club on a daily basis and could be found there, without fail, every day between the hours of a quarter to five and twenty past eight.

It was an unusually warm fall day and dusk had already begun as Holmes and I walked arm in arm down the crowded sidewalks of the city, passing by all the inhabitants that came our way. Holmes would occasionally deduce the trade of those we would encounter in this manner, but today I saw his brow knitted in concentration and his eyes fiery with anticipation of discussing the case with his brother.

Once upon St. James we saw Pall Mall hove into view and crossed over to it. It was only a short walk from there to the Diogenes Club. Holmes left me in the Stranger's Room and went in search of his brother. I seated myself in a well-upholstered chair and perused the latest issue of Punch. I had not gotten through the first page when Holmes reappeared with his brother.

Mycroft Holmes was alike and yet not alike to his brother. Facially there was an undeniable resemblance, most especially about the alert and intelligent eyes, but in body type Mycroft was the polar opposite of the trim and spare Holmes. He was a fleshy man, over six feet in height, and moved with a ponderous reluctance that advertised his sedentary nature. Holmes had always made it a point to explain to me that Mycroft possessed the same gift of deduction that he enjoyed and to a greater degree. I was somewhat reluctant to believe this, but as false modesty was not a trait that my old friend evinced in any measure, I was inclined to believe him. Mycroft crossed the room and held out a fleshy hand to me. I shook it and he lowered his bulk into a seat adjacent to mine and sat in repose.

"I suppose, Sherlock, that this visit means you are out of your depths again," he said through hooded and languid eyelids.

Mycroft was the elder brother by some seven years and I had noted on previous occasions that he had a distinctly paternal manner of speaking to his younger sibling. Holmes merely smiled at the slight superiority of tone his brother employed.

"Now, Mycroft, you do not seriously suggest that I have never on any occasion visited you without ulterior motive?"

"Of course not, my boy," said Mycroft. "And in any case, I enjoy the intellectual challenge of a mysterious case as much as do you. It is only that I am not inclined to race about the country to prove my theories correct. Indeed, Sherlock, you have been given more than your share of intellect and prowess and I daresay you only require my aid in times of great need. Now tell me. Is there a case at hand?"

In answer Holmes drew a sheaf of papers from his jacket pocket.

"So it's the Masterson counterfeiting case, is it," he stated rather than asked. "I had thought you might be around with that one, Sherlock."

Holmes read the question on my face.

"My dear doctor, Mycroft was able to deduce that it was on the Masterson case by the simple fact that it was he who suggested that the Crown seek my help in the matter."

"That is so," said the brother. "Of course, it could have been another case which brought you here, but from the seal on the top document I perceive the signature, forged of course, of Sir Arthur Brisbane. That knight of the realm is at the heart of this conspiracy."

The brothers began conversing in low tones about the matter at hand. They made no effort to hide their conversation from me, but in a matter of minutes I found myself quite at sea. They were jumping from subject to subject and using the most baffling terms and acronyms that it was impossible for me to follow.

I observed that Holmes was growing in eagerness as, I assumed, they drew closer to a possible avenue towards the completion of the task. Mycroft, however, evinced none of the enthusiasm of his brother. To him each task was as alike to another and he treated each as mere intellectual moot trials.

As the discussion drew somewhat more animated, at least from my friend, the details grew less easy to follow. At length I decided to stretch my legs and I wandered to the window and looked out upon the street. The two great minds took no notice of my leaving, if they even recalled that I was present, and continued on in their baffling discussion. While I was standing at the window I saw a hansom pull to the curb in front of the club and behind me I heard the voice of my friend.

"Of course, Mycroft," he cried. "Masterson must route his booty through Scotland and then to America."

"And of course, you now realize how he can be stopped," said the brother blandly.

"Naturally," replied Holmes

"The green ink being the key, of course," said Mycroft.

"Of course. There could be no other

explanation."

As the brothers were sagely nodding their heads and agreeing that the solution was in hand, I saw a page come in with a note on a platter. He walked up to the seated Mycroft and presented him with the note. The fleshy man read the note and handed it without interest to my friend. Holmes looked the note over twice. He exchanged a glance with his brother and looked over to me.

"There has been murder, Doctor, and our help is requested."

CHAPTER TWO

*H*e thrust the note towards me. It was a short message, addressed to Holmes, from Inspector Stanley Hopkins. Young Hopkins was a favorite of Holmes's, and he in turn idolized the great detective. The message simply stated that a murder had been committed on Lambs Lane and that Hopkins wished Holmes to come to the scene immediately. Apparently the message had gone to Baker Street at first and then had been forwarded to the Diogenes Club by the redoubtable Mrs. Hudson.

"It would appear that your protégé requires the assistance of the master," I observed.

"So it would seem," said Holmes. "But how can I abandon the Masterson case at this crucial point? Hopkins shall have to strive for success on his own this time. He is quite capable."

"Sherlock, you do me an injustice," cried Mycroft.

"How so?" asked Holmes.

"Why, surely at this point in the Masterson

affair the energetic sibling can give way to his more tranquil brother. I assure you that I will carry the ball forward to the end."

I could plainly see the doubt play out upon the countenance of my friend. The elder Holmes seemed blithely unaware of the lack of confidence his brother had in him And I, as well, was doubtful of the ability of Mycroft Holmes to finish any task that required great effort.

"You are certain that you can finish this business?" Holmes asked at last.

"But of certainty," said Mycroft loftily. "I will inform the Admiralty to stop *The Gadfly* at once before she leaves port. We are agreed that *The Gadfly* is the only possible ship Masterson could choose?"

"Naturally," replied my friend. Holmes once more hesitated before he continued. "If you are certain, then I will leave it in your capable hands."

"Let the matter pass from your mind, Sherlock, but return to inform me of how this case plays out. I have not your energetic nature, but I enjoy unraveling a riddle as much as you do. Now, off with you. I can see that you are straining at the leash."

The metaphor was an unflattering one, but I deemed it an accurate portrait of Holmes and we quickly exited the club. Once we were on the street, the doorman blew his whistle for a cab.

"I must confess I am unacquainted with Lambs Lane, Holmes," I said. "Where away is it?"

I knew that the detective carried within his brain an encyclopedic imprint of the streets of London, and I was confident that he knew exactly where the message from Hopkins had originated. I was not disappointed when he made a quick reply to my question.

"Lambs Lane is a quiet road on the northern outskirts of London, Doctor. The address given is, I believe, a section of the lane that is largely uninhabited save for a few scattered cottages."

Our hansom arrived and Holmes and I entered. Holmes gave the address to the driver. I had expected that the driver would have needed additional directions, but I did not account for the Knowledge. The man simply tipped his tweed cap at Holmes's order, and with a flick of his whip, the hansom clattered down the street to our destination.

We rode in silence as our cab traveled through avenues that became less and less crowded with traffic. We finally found ourselves on a somewhat lonely stretch of road and I perceived by my friend's increased excitement that we were drawing near to our destination. The hansom finally came to an abrupt halt and I peered out the window.

We had stopped in front of a picturesque cottage that stood well back from the road. The cottage was obviously the murder scene. It was well lit, and I noted several carriages and police personnel were in front of the home. We alighted, and Holmes instructed the driver to await our return. I noted that several coins passed from Holmes to the man, and he happily acceded to Holmes's request. Holmes took me by the arm, and together we went up the cobbled walk to the cottage.

The location, as Holmes had stated, was one of few residences. The cottage we had been drawn to had one near neighbor to the west and one much further away to the south. There was another cottage almost directly across from it, but that dwelling appeared to be in a state of advanced dilapidation and I doubted that it held any occupants. Other than those homes, the rest of the visible road was dark and gloomy, though I allowed that the fact that I knew a murder victim lay within had clouded my judgment.

As we approached the front entrance, I perceived a stolid police sergeant on duty. While I did not recognize him, he certainly knew of Sherlock Holmes and he immediately admitted us to the residence.

The heavy front door opened onto a foyer. The foyer had an ornate Chinese rug as its primary decoration, with a small table to one side with a lamp and a vase. Directly in front of the table lay the body of a dead woman.

"Ah, Mr. Holmes," cried Inspector Hopkins as he spied the figure of the detective. The Inspector came from what was obviously the sitting room of the home. There were several more police officers in the room with him as well as two men in civilian dress and one woman. They remained behind as Inspector Hopkins joined Holmes and myself in the foyer.

The Inspector was a man of some thirty years. He was of middle height, dark, and had a thick mustache, but was otherwise clean shaven. He vigorously shook hands with Holmes and myself and turned a rueful eye towards the corpse.

The body was that of a woman. She appeared to be in her late twenties to early thirties. She had been a beautiful woman in life, I observed, with fair hair and a fair complexion. The woman had a slim figure and fine skin, but savage damage had been done to her. She had been struck in the back of the head with some sort of blunt instrument, as was attested to by a wound that had bled somewhat. The blood was still wet in appearance, but had not pooled on the floor. She was wearing a black blouse more appropriate for mourning, which was buttoned up to nearly her chin in a style that had been popular years before. Her dress and hair were very stylish except for that. She was obviously a woman who had paid great attention to her appearance. The black blouse she wore was perforated by a cruel rend in the upper torso.

The dagger that had struck the blow was next to the body. It was a thick kitchen blade that had been thrown to the floor by either the assailant or by the woman herself in her death throes. The blow to the head had obviously been delivered with a candlestick that was also lying on the floor of the foyer.

"As you can see, Mr. Holmes, the lady has been murdered in a most violent fashion," said Hopkins.

Holmes knelt by the body and began to examine it closely. The wound on the head drew his attention first. He pulled his glass from his pocket and employed it upon the wound area. I heard a satisfied grunt from him, and he turned his attention to the knife wound. The room was well lit, and despite the dark color of the woman's shirt, I could see that the area around the wound was still wet with what must have been blood. This meant, of course, that the crime was a recent one. I noted that Holmes delicately placed his finger on the shirt next to the wound and brought it to his nose. I could not ascertain what he hoped to accomplish with this, but I watched him closely as did the young Inspector.

The detective then placed a finger to the woman's closed eyelids and raised one gently. Rigor had not yet set in, and the lid lifted easily in his grasp. He performed this same operation on the other eye. I could see that both eyes were shot through with blood.

Holmes next turned his attention to the hands of the woman. He again employed the magnifying glass, turning the hands over several times, and he seemed particularly interested in her fingers. Holmes finally seemed satisfied that the body had given up what clues it contained, and he arose slowly from the corpse.

"You have noted the hands of the woman, of course," he said to Hopkins.

"Why, nothing out of the ordinary, Mr. Holmes," said Hopkins. "She has no defensive wounds, if that is what you mean."

I bent down to take a close look at the woman's hands myself. They were small and without blemish. They were the hands of a woman at leisure for certain. The nails were well manicured. They were, however, much shorter than I preferred on a woman, but they were perfectly rounded as women learn to do from childhood. As I arose Holmes continued his conversation with the Inspector.

"I take it that the police surgeon has examined the body," said he, as he absentmindedly picked up the lamp for a moment.

"That is so, sir," replied Hopkins. "He would not commit himself to cause of death. Either injury may have been fatal. It will all come out in the coroner's inquest though it has little impact upon our investigation. It was obviously murder in any case."

"Pray give me all the details, Hopkins," ordered Holmes, as he sat the lamp back down on the table. "Begin with the identity of the woman."

Hopkins pulled a battered notebook from his jacket and opened it.

"The lady is Miss Anne Benton," began Hopkins in an officious manner. "She is 31 years of age and lives in this cottage with her brother, a Mr. William Benton. The two are leasing this house through the spring from Harold Highlander."

"The shipping magnate?" I inquired.

"The very one, Doctor," said Hopkins with a smile. "That is the man himself in the sitting room."

Hopkins gestured towards a grey-haired man standing erect by the fireplace. The light from the flames cast a shadow across one half of his face. He was a very tall and slender man that I estimated to be in his mid-sixties. He was clean shaven and looked to be well composed despite the death of his tenant.

"The others are the nearest neighbors of the dead woman," said Hopkins. "The elderly gentleman is Simon Langston. He is a retired tailor. I understand he had a very nice business, when he sold out and bought the cottage across the street."

I was momentarily shocked that anyone was presently residing in the dilapidated cottage I had seen on the way in. Whatever fortune the old man had had upon retirement had certainly not gone into home upkeep. I glanced into the sitting room again and saw a wizened old man seated in an armchair, paying attention to no one. He appeared to be almost asleep and was leaning slightly to one side.

"The woman is Elizabeth Woodbury. She lives next door to the deceased woman. She was the second person on the scene after Mr. Highlander."

Again Hopkins nodded towards the knot of people in the next room. As the others were all men, there was no mystery as to the identity of Elizabeth Woodbury. She was a tall woman with striking red hair. I judged her to be thirty, but she was well preserved and indeed a fine figure of a woman. She had alabaster skin and was wearing a grey blouse with a plaid skirt. It was an odd combination, but was pleasing to the eye for some reason. I perceived that Holmes's eyes were upon me. He followed my gaze and smiled.

"She is a lovely woman, Doctor," he said.

"What's that, Holmes?" I asked. "Oh, yes. Miss Woodbury is quite lovely."

"This lady must have been thought of as beautiful as well."

I looked down at the body of Miss Benton and grimaced. Holmes believed, or pretended to believe, that I was easily led astray by a pretty face and a pleasing figure. Normally I would admonish him for such thinking and protest my innocence, but I regretted that it was true in this instance. The figure of Miss Woodbury had, in fact, temporarily driven the murder from my mind in spite of the fact that the corpse lay within sight. I hoped that no one save Holmes had noticed. With a slight cough Hopkins proceeded.

"At any rate, Mr. Highlander came by the cottage at five o'clock and no one answered his knock. He was alarmed and tried to enter, but found that the door was bolted. He created enough ruckus that Miss Woodbury became alarmed at the noise and joined him. Together they found the side door open. They entered and found the deceased."

He halted for a moment and I saw the shrewd eyes of Sherlock Holmes upon him.

"I have two questions, Hopkins," he began. "Firstly, why did Mr. Highlander become so concerned so quickly when no one answered the door? And secondly, why did you call me in so quickly on what seems to be a very ordinary crime?"

Hopkins met Holmes's eyes and answered directly.

"The answer to each question is the same, sir," he said. "Mr. Highlander had received a note informing him that Miss Benton would be murdered at five o'clock today."

CHAPTER THREE

*I*n spite of my long association with Holmes, and the association with crime that had come with it, I found myself shocked at the words of the Inspector and a thrill ran through me.

"What's this you say?" exclaimed Holmes.

"Most extraordinary," said I.

"It is so," stated Hopkins with a bit of a smile on his face. As the student, he was enjoying surprising the master. "Mr. Highlander has testified that he received this note at just on five today."

Hopkins pulled a small sheet of notepaper from his pocket and handed it to Holmes.

"Five o'clock, you say, and it is just on seven right now," said Holmes, peering at the note.

As I was standing next to him, I could see it easily. It was written in pencil in a masculine hand. It read as follows:

You can't save her. Anne Benton dies at five for

her sins.

Holmes looked grimly from the note to the Inspector.

"You say Mr. Highlander received this note. In what manner did he receive it?"

"He declares that it was pushed through the mail slot with the rest of his correspondence. It was sitting atop the pile."

"And what of the post mark on the envelope?"

"There was no envelope, Mr. Holmes. The sheet of paper was merely on the floor with the rest of the mail."

"So it is possible that it was placed there later, though certainly not earlier if it was on top of the other mail."

"Yes, that would follow," said Hopkins thoughtfully.

"Has the postman been questioned as of yet?" asked Holmes.

"Not as of yet, Mr. Holmes. The murder is only two hours old, and I have been on the scene for less than an hour myself. I have sent instructions to have the man located, though."

"That is well," said Holmes. "How many entrances are there to the cottage?"

"Three, sir," replied Hopkins. "The front door and the rear door were both bolted. Miss Woodbury and Mr. Highlander came in through the side door, as I have said. That door was open."

"And that door faces Miss Woodbury's cottage, I take it."

"That is so."

"That seems clear."

"I know your methods, Mr. Holmes, and I have preserved the scene as much as possible for your inspection."

"Capital, Hopkins! Let us then examine the side door for clues. If the other two doors were bolted from the inside, then the killer must have escaped through that door."

Hopkins saw the logic of that immediately, and he ushered Holmes and myself towards the sitting room. Hopkins gave a nod to those seated and standing in the room and swept past them. The doorway that we were seeking ran off of a small anteroom that was adjacent to the sitting room.

The side entrance was a set of French doors that

looked strangely ornate for the cottage. They opened outward onto a patio that consisted of a single, very large, flagstone. The stone served as a small patio. The stone butted up directly to the house and was surrounded on the remaining sides by a three foot wide border of earth that gave way to a finely cared for lawn. A rake and a spade were leaning against the home as testament to the work that went into the well-tended grounds.

Holmes was drawn to the sandy border of the flagstone. Most of it was finely raked and even, but there were footprints clearly visible as well.

"Have your men been through here, Hopkins?" demanded Holmes.

"No, sir," he replied. "They are as you see them now. My men are well trained, and they were careful to preserve this until I arrived. I, in turn, preserved it until you could examine it."

Holmes merely nodded in answer. There were two clear sets of footprints going into the house. One set was a large footprint even for a man. As Harold Highlander was a tall man, I took those prints to be his. The other set was much smaller and undoubtedly belonged to Miss Woodbury.

"What do you see here, Hopkins?" asked Holmes.

"The footprints of two people entering the cottage," he said cautiously.

"Indeed," replied my friend. "Anything else?"

"Only that they belong to the two people who discovered the body."

"Undoubtedly, but there is also someone leaving as you can see by close study," said Holmes.

Hopkins stepped forward and looked to the area Holmes had indicated. For a few moments he was rigidly still as he examined the ground. Presently a low whistle escaped from his lips.

"I believe you are right, Mr. Holmes," he said finally. "It is nearly obliterated by the one on top, but I do see it plainly now that you point it out."

I followed the man's eyes and the glint of an outline appeared to me as well. The footprint was somewhat smaller than Harold Highlander's and much larger than the prints left by Elizabeth Woodbury. The single print was going away from the cottage.

"As you can see here, Hopkins," said Holmes in a lecturing tone, "Mr. Highlander has stepped on top of the earlier print. As the earlier print is a bit deeper, the faint outline remains. A pity that it was disturbed, as it may have yielded further clues as to the identity of the person."

Hopkins noticed a slight emphasis on the last sentence and pounced.

"Mr. Holmes, are you implying that Mr. Highlander stepped on the print on purpose?"

"Nothing of the sort, Hopkins. It was already dark when he arrived and he and Miss Woodbury were hurrying. No, I believe it was happenstance, but unfortunate nonetheless. You have noted that Miss Woodbury left two prints and Mr. Highlander and the other man left only one each."

"Yes, sir. You are implying that the fact that there is only one outgoing print means it was left by a man, since the stride of most men is longer than that of most women."

"You are coming along, Hopkins. That is well stated, although the depth of the print also shows the weight of a man. I suppose there is a gardener," said Holmes.

"There is, sir. I have found that Miss Woodbury and the deceased employed the same man. He comes two days a week. He was last here the day before yesterday."

"I find that most interesting," said Holmes

almost to himself.

The Inspector said nothing in reply and made several notes on his pad.

"Surely you will wish to speak with Miss Woodbury and Mr. Highlander," I said to Holmes.

"Why, Doctor, you have read my very thoughts," said Holmes. "Hopkins, if you will be so kind as to lead us."

We three walked back into the sitting room, and Inspector Hopkins made the introductions. Both men approached us and shook hands with Holmes and myself. The hands of Harold Highlander were large, but soft. These were not hands used to labor. Simon Langston's grip was surprisingly strong, given his age; his hands were well calloused and his nails were dirty. To my surprise, Miss Woodbury arose at the introduction and also shook hands with the two of us. She had a firm and brisk grip. I saw that her nails were nicely manicured and much longer than the deceased's, in the style that I preferred for ladies. I also saw upon closer inspection that her alabaster skin was owed, at least partially, to the fact that her face was heavily powdered. Many ladies of the upper crust powdered their faces in that manner, and on her it was quite striking. She, and the elderly tailor, resumed their respective seats following the introduction, while Harold Highlander remained standing. He appeared to be moved to speak. After a moment he did so, although he addressed Holmes directly instead of the Inspector. I had noticed in the past the tendency of people to become overawed in Holmes's presence, so this came as no surprise to me, and Hopkins showed no offense.

"This is a terrible tragedy for one so young, Mr. Holmes," said Highlander. "The poor girl had her entire life before her."

"As do we all, Mr. Highlander," Holmes wryly observed. "Did you know the lady well, sir?"

"I am afraid I did not," said the man.

"Come now, sir. That can hardly be true," said Holmes.

"Now just one moment, Mr. Holmes," said Highlander in protest. "I have some idea of your reputation, but if you are implying an improper relationship with the lady, you are mistaken."

"I was implying nothing of the sort, Mr. Highlander."

"Well, then, that is all right," said Highlander gruffly. "I apologize if I lost my temper. I pride myself upon remaining cool under fire, as they say."

An uneasy silence grew, as Holmes made no

further statement. Hopkins finally stirred himself to address Holmes.

"Sir, I do not understand this," he began. "You tell Mr. Highlander that you were not implying an improper relationship, but you state that his denial of knowing the lady well is false. How can both be true?"

Hopkins had a point, and I looked to the great man for his reply, but none seemed to be forthcoming. Highlander was shaking his head. He had an expression on his face that seemed to say that perhaps the reputation of Sherlock Holmes was overstated. He was obviously dubious of the great detective.

"There is one point that seems to have been overlooked up until now," said Holmes. "Mr. Highlander claims only a passing acquaintance with the lady, yet at least one person believes that he knows her well and cares about her."

"Why is that?" asked Hopkins mystified.

"Why else would he have been sent the note?" said Holmes.

CHAPTER FOUR

"I have been a fool to overlook that, Mr. Holmes," said Hopkins in a chastened tone. "What of that point, Mr. Highlander?"

"I don't quite follow you, Inspector," said he.

"Come now, sir. That simply will not do. Why was this note delivered to you?"

"I suppose that it was delivered to me because this is my cottage," said Highlander. "It can be for no other reason. I knew very little of the woman or her brother. To my knowledge, they were strangers to England before they let this home."

"Someone knew the lady well enough to commit murder," observed Holmes.

"Quite, quite," said Highlander. "Perhaps her brother can tell you more when he returns."

"Where is he?" asked the Inspector. "Does anyone know?"

"He is away looking for work as an estate

agent," said Elizabeth Woodbury. "Anne told me yesterday that he would be away until tomorrow."

"That is so," chimed in Simon Langston. "I saw the lad leave myself. He has been away often since they have arrived. The poor sister has been alone mostly."

I gave the old man a sidelong glance. There was intimation in his voice of something untoward, I thought, but he said nothing else on the subject.

"Let us leave aside the reason the note was given to you, Mr. Highlander, at least for the moment," said Holmes. "How exactly did the lady come to lease this particular cottage?"

"Her brother answered an advertisement some six months ago," said Highlander. "He came to my home. I reside a mile or so up the lane. I showed him the cottage that same day. He found the home and the terms satisfactory and we signed the necessary paperwork. It was quite ordinary."

"Was the sister with him?" asked Holmes.

"Not at that time. As I understood it Mr. William Benton had recently been invalided out of the army from service in India. He had come over first to arrange housing, and she was to follow after she settled affairs in India."

"What of their people? Do they have any relatives in England?"

"I did not inquire, Mr. Holmes. I admit I assumed that the parents were deceased as he and the sister were living together, but that is mere surmise."

I saw Miss Woodbury nodding her head.

"That is how I understood matters as well," said she. "Anne said that she and William were alone in the world. They were very attached to one another."

"Very well," said Holmes. "But surely, Mr. Highlander, you at some point met Miss Benton."

"Of course, sir," he said with irritation. "I never claimed to be a stranger to the lady. We had the two of them over for bridge and the like on several occasions."

"Who exactly do you mean when you say 'we' had them over? Your wife and yourself, I suppose."

"No, Mr. Holmes, I am a widower. My household consists of my son David and his wife Sylvia. The young people were all of the same approximate age, so it was natural to have the Bentons over from time to time."

"I am surprised that your son and daughter-in-law did not socialize more with the deceased and her brother," ventured Holmes.

"Well, in fact, they did," conceded Harold Highlander. "David and William have gone riding together, and I believe that Sylvia was in the habit of coming over for tea occasionally."

"So, in fact, they were closer to the Bentons than yourself?"

Highlander merely shrugged his shoulders in response.

"And if that is true, then the note could have been meant for either your son or his wife, and not you," said Holmes.

Highlander reacted as if that thought had not occurred to him.

"I suppose that is possible," he said reluctantly. "I just took it for granted that it was meant for me."

"Just so," said Holmes. "When precisely did you first notice the note?"

"It was just past five. I remember because I heard the clock chime, and it reminded me to check the mail."

"What did you do then?"

"At first I did nothing," he said slowly. "I thought it was a joke, and a damned poor one, but as I reflected upon it I began to grow uneasy. I decided to see the lady and satisfy myself that nothing untoward had happened."

You left your home when, would you say?"

"It must have been only a few minutes past five. I hurried along the lane-"

"Do you mean to say that you came on foot?" interrupted Holmes. "Surely if you were worried, you would have ridden."

"I have not been astride a horse in many years, Mr. Holmes. A man of my age must yield to the passing years."

"Yet a brisk walk was not out of the question."

"It is only a mile, or so, as I say. I can certainly manage that distance on foot," replied the man with some dignity.

"But if you were alarmed, surely you could have sent your son or a servant."

"I was not alarmed, Mr. Holmes. I merely wanted to satisfy my own curiosity. I did not want to rouse the entire house because of an anonymous note among the mail."

I thought that the man's attitude was quite in

keeping with the character of the stolid Englishman of his class. Holmes must have felt the same way as he waited for the man to continue.

"As I was saying," Highlander went on, with a bit of reproach in his voice. "When I arrived I came up the walk and knocked upon the door. When it was not answered, I fear that I did allow the wind to get up into me a bit. I knocked louder and louder until Miss Woodbury came over to see what all the fuss was about."

"That is so," said the lady. "Mr. Highlander was very agitated by the time I arrived."

"Were you acquainted with Mr. Highlander before this episode?" asked Holmes.

"Oh, indeed yes. Father and he knew each other a bit. We both use the same bank, and, after all, he has owned the cottage next door for many years."

"Then you must know the son as well," said Holmes.

The lady nodded and I thought I detected some color come into her cheeks despite the powder on them. I sensed a possible romantic attachment between her and the son, perhaps in years past. I made a note to myself to mention the possibility to Holmes in case it might prove pertinent to the crime.

"At any rate," continued Highlander. "I tried the door and found it was bolted. Miss Woodbury suggested we try the side door."

"Why did you do that, Miss Woodbury? Mr. Highlander had a reason to worry about the lady, but she may have merely been out. Why did you suggest trying other doors? Had you been told by Mr. Highlander about the note?"

"At that point I knew nothing of the note, sir. The reason I became worried is that I knew that Anne was home. She had been out in the yard earlier. I had spoken to her, and I had not seen her leave."

"Quite rightly so," said Highlander as he patted her on the forearm. "We found that the door opened, and we entered the house. There were no lights, but the fire had been lit, and it illuminated the room enough for us to see the body."

"Oh, yes, it was obvious that she had passed, the poor dear."

Elizabeth Woodbury began to sniffle at her own words, and I feared that she would collapse in a fit. I reached to my sleeve for a handkerchief, but she gathered herself, bravely I thought, and continued.

"Mr. Highlander, bless him, took control of matters at that point," she said. "I am afraid I was quite insensible with shock at the time."

"That is so," said Harold Highlander somewhat importantly. "I looked around the cottage to see if anyone was still lurking about, but I found nothing. I then ran into the lane with the intention of finding help. Mr. Langston was just coming out of his front door at the time. I was about to inform him of events, when I spied a constable some hundred yards down the lane. It was Providence that put him there. I hallooed at him, and he came on a run. He took charge of the matter and began blowing his whistle. Within what seemed like minutes, several more constables answered the call, and then the Inspector was called for. I must say that London has the finest police in the island. Even here on the outskirts, an officer is only a call away."

"That is told in a very straightforward manner," said Holmes. "Now, Mr. Langston, how do you come into this tale?"

The grizzled, retired gentleman rubbed his chin with one grimy hand.

"It is as Highlander has said, Mr. Holmes. I have already told all of this to the Inspector."

"Indulge me, Mr. Langston," said Holmes with a smile. "I wish to hear it from you directly, if you do not mind."

"I suppose I get your meaning," he said. "I rather like getting it from the horse's mouth myself."

The old man had a good laugh at his joke, and it was some few moments before he mastered himself enough to continue.

"I was in my sitting room reading until about four o'clock today, when I must have fallen asleep in my chair. When you're of my age it will happen to you too, my lads. But, anyway, I was awoken at sometime after five by someone pounding on the door of the Benton cottage. My sitting room has windows that face the lane, and I saw a person I later found to be Highlander knocking on the door very persistently. Presently Miss Woodbury came over, and I watched as they went around to the side. After a few minutes I saw lamps being lit, and then Highlander dashed into the lane. I came out to find what all the fuss was about."

"How long have you been retired, Mr. Langston?" asked Holmes.

Langston seemed surprised by the question.

"It has been almost six years now."

"I suppose you spend much of your time in your sitting room, observing life. As a tradesman, you know the nature of people better than most, I would wager."

"You look to flatter me and insult me at the same time, Mr. Holmes," said the old man with a grin. "You imagine that an old man, such as myself, is the neighborhood snoop. Is that it?"

"Nothing of the sort," said Holmes in protest. "But still, I think little gets by you."

Simon Langston made no response, but I saw again a shrewd flash loom in his eyes. Simon Langston was no one's fool, I thought.

Holmes had wandered over by the fire, and I saw him gazing into it intently. The fire had largely died out by this point in the evening. The lamps were all lit now so the light from the fire was not needed. I watched as my friend walked over to the nearly dead fire. I watched him as he crouched down without saying a word to anyone else. He grabbed a set of tongs sitting next to the hearth and reached into the ashes. He poked around for some moments and then withdrew the tongs. He held them in front of him and blew on the end. Presently he dropped something into his hands and walked back to the group.

"What is it that you have found?" asked Hopkins.

In answer Holmes showed all of us a small brass button.

"Why, that is odd!" exclaimed Hopkins. "Dashed lucky that you should have spied out such a thing."

"It was not luck," answered the great detective. "You see, Hopkins, I was looking for it."

CHAPTER FIVE

"**W**hat?" cried Inspector Hopkins. "How could you know such a thing, sir?"

"It was an obvious deduction," said Holmes blandly. "In point of fact, I believe you will find more such buttons remaining in the ashes."

"How did they come to be in the ashes?" asked Hopkins.

"They are in the ashes for the simple reason that the fireplace does not achieve a high enough temperature to reach the melting point of brass. On the other hand, cloth burns easily."

"Do you mean to say, Holmes, that a piece of clothing has been placed in the fire and the buttons are all that remain of the garment?" asked I.

"That is precisely what I mean, Doctor. Miss Woodbury and Mr. Highlander both testified that the fire was burning brightly when they came in the side door. Brightly enough in fact, that it illuminated the room. This can only mean that the fire was built a short time prior to their entrance. Otherwise it would have died down before they came in."

Holmes never failed to amaze me with his powers of observation. I was frankly proud of my friend for yet another demonstration of his abilities, but I saw doubt upon the face of Inspector Stanley Hopkins. The Inspector, of course, greatly admired Holmes, but it was obvious that he had difficulty in subscribing to Holmes's view.

"I see several problems with your theory, Mr. Holmes," he said finally.

"Indeed," said Holmes. "Pray unburden yourself, Hopkins."

"I hesitate to gainsay you, sir, but I can advance several problems with your thinking. Firstly, the fire could be complete happenstance. It may have been the lady herself who felt a chill and built the fire for warmth. Secondly, these buttons you have found may have been in the ash heap for days, even weeks, before today. They may have nothing to do with the crime."

As Hopkins was speaking, I saw that one of the sergeants was sifting through the still-hot ashes. He had found, as Homes had predicted, another dozen or so of the same style brass buttons. The man brought them over and silently set them upon a table in front of the Inspector.

"I believe that I can set your thinking straight," said Holmes. "In the case of your first objection, I believe that it is highly unlikely that the lady built the fire herself, although it is possible. The day had been unseasonably warm. Indeed, even into the evening it is still quite comfortable. Therefore, I think that the killer was the person who laid in the fire for a purpose. As to your second point, I must accuse you of sloppy logic and observation, Hopkins. Look about the room. This is a well-cared-for home and Miss Benton was not the sort of person to let ashes pile up in the grate. Look at the fireplace. The ashes that are there are obviously the ashes of a single fire only. The idea that several fires were built and that the buttons have been among the ashes for an indeterminate length of time is pure folly."

I could see Hopkins visibly wilt and wince at the harsh words of Sherlock Holmes. Langston smirked at what I thought was his endorsement of the older man, Holmes, giving the younger man a stern lesson. Hopkins took in the tongue-lashing and set a firm chin.

"Only a fool would argue the point with you any longer, Mr. Holmes," he said. "That being the case, I must accept your theory. I believe that I can, with your permission, flesh it out a bit further."

"By all means," said Holmes with a nod.

"As I see it, the murderer must have splashed

blood upon his, or her, shirt during the murder. The killer panics. The bloody shirt is tantamount to a confession to a capital crime. Then the idea hits. The household consists of both a man and a woman, so no matter what the gender of the killer, extra clothing is available. The killer changes and thrusts the bloody, incriminating, garment into the fire leaving only the buttons, which will likely be overlooked."

"Indeed would have been overlooked, save for Holmes," said I.

"Agreed, Doctor," said Hopkins with a rueful smile. "Though I believe that I, at the very least, demonstrated acumen in calling for the assistance of him. What say you, Mr. Holmes? Do you agree with my thinking?"

"It is certainly one possibility, but the most likely one, well..."

Holmes trailed off and walked over to a desk that stood in the corner of the sitting room. I followed him with my eyes, as he seemed to take great interest in the area. Hopkins had seized upon his extension of Holmes's theory and continued, oblivious to the wanderings of my friend.

"This is actually quite marvelous," said he. "Once Mr. William Benton returns, we may be able to narrow the field a good deal."

"How is that, Inspector?" I asked with genuine curiosity.

"It is simplicity itself, Doctor," he returned, borrowing one of Holmes's pet phrases. "It is obvious that we cannot question Miss Benton as to whether one of her blouses is missing, but we can question Mr. Benton as to any missing items from his wardrobe."

"I see," said I. "And if he has a missing shirt, then the killer is a man; and if not, then the killer must be a woman. That is well thought out, Inspector."

"I merely apply the methods of Mr. Holmes. Once we establish the gender of the killer, we can begin to identify suspects. Is that not the next logical step, Mr. Holmes?"

"What's that?" asked Holmes as he looked up from the desk. "Oh, yes. I suppose that is a useful endeavor."

Elizabeth Woodbury had been growing increasingly agitated during this particular discussion and could finally no longer restrain herself.

"Are you actually suggesting that some man killed poor Anne, and while she lay dead upon the floor, he coolly went into William's bedchamber and took one of his shirts, and then built a fire and cast the bloody one into it? Why, Macbeth was never half so cruel as that.

What kind of man would do such a thing?"

"I've seen many more years than you have, Miss Woodbury," stated Simon Langston. "I speak to you now as a Dutch uncle, when I say that the cruelty of man to his fellow being is unbounded by nature or religion."

These were sage words, but I must confess that I wondered where a mere tailor, a respectable trade to be certain, might have come across such acts of cruelty as to be such a harsh judge of the human condition.

"Are you quite alone in the world, Mr. Langston?" asked Holmes from the desk.

The question seemed to come from nowhere in particular, but the old man replied readily enough.

"I had one son, sir. Jacob was his name."

"And what became of him?" asked Holmes gently.

"He served the Crown faithfully in the army, Mr. Holmes, he did. He gave his life in the awful fight with the Boers in South Africa."

"Killed in action, then," said Holmes.

"Yes, he was killed in the Transvaal by one of their damn commando raiders. Will-o-the-wisps they were, sir. They had mutilated his body by the time it was recovered. That is what men are capable of, you see."

"I never knew that, Mr. Langston," said Miss Woodbury. "I am so sorry for you. That is a lot of pain to carry."

"You are very kind, Miss Woodbury. I would never have told such a story in mixed company were it not for the horrible circumstances. It is a story I share with few people. Now, Mr. William Benton being a soldier himself, I did unburden to once. He was a sympathetic ear for an old man."

"This will be a heavy burden on him when he is told," observed Elizabeth Woodbury. "It is all such a nightmare."

"Not a nightmare, Miss Woodbury," said Holmes. "This is all too real. And to return to your point about a man doing all this in cold blood, I remind you that there is another alternative."

"What is that, Mr. Holmes?"

"Why, simply that the killer may have been a woman. Any woman of the same approximate size as Miss Benton might have donned one of her blouses with no one the wiser. Why, someone your size for instance."

"If you are attempting to bait me, Mr. Holmes, you will not succeed," said the lady with a grim smile.

"My own father died in my arms from illness just last year, so I have seen something of death before. However, if you are insinuating that I stabbed Anne and then put on the clothing of a dead woman, you are mistaken."

"I insinuate nothing, but I want everyone here to understand the gravity of the situation," said Holmes. "There has been murder done here today, and it was a most cruel murder at that, if such a thing can be measured. Everyone with even the most tangential connection with the woman is under suspicion. Is that not right, Hopkins?"

"You speak the truth, sir."

"I draw your attention to the fact that both Miss Woodbury and Mr. Langston were alone all afternoon and have no one to vouchsafe for their innocence."

"Now see here, young man," began Simon Langston, but Holmes waved him away.

"And, Mr. Highlander, I believe that you claim to have been alone in your study for most of the time in question before you found the note."

"That is so," said Highlander. "I claim no special alibi. I was alone."

"Precisely. And your son and his wife are

intimates of the Bentons. Where are they, and where have they been, to your knowledge?"

"I think you can safely put them out of this, Mr. Holmes. My son, David, went riding earlier in the day."

"Alone?" asked Holmes.

"Yes, alone, but he must have been seen by many people."

"Quite possibly. And what of your daughter-in-law?"

"Sylvia was shopping in the West End. She was alone as well, but, my goodness, many people must have observed her as well and can attest to her absence from this district."

"I am certain that is true, and I meant to cast no aspersions, but alibis are often not what they first appear to be. Why, you yourself, Mr. Highlander, may have been here earlier in the day and yet still deny it now, even were you not guilty."

"Why on earth would an innocent man do such a thing?" asked Highlander incredulously.

"Why, simply to avoid suspicion. It happens very frequently, I assure you. This has been your experience as well, has it not, Hopkins?"

"Oh yes, sir. It is maddening, but people do not think it through and will oftentimes hold back something in a murder investigation."

"Not only that," said Holmes. "But there are often maddening coincidences in a case such as this. For example, Hopkins, do you have the note Mr. Highlander received?"

"Right here, sir."

"May I see it again, please?"

Hopkins strode over to the desk where Holmes was still standing, and I followed in his wake with curiosity. Holmes held the note in his hand and examined it for a moment before he spoke.

"Yes, it is just as I thought," he said. "Hopkins, tell me what you see on the desk."

"Why, nothing out of the ordinary, sir. A blotter, an inkwell, a pen, several pencils, a notepad, and letters addressed to Mr. William Benton."

"I draw your attention to the fact that the notepad on the desk and the sheet of note paper with the warning on it are of the same size."

"Well, that is a coincidence, sir," Hopkins conceded. "But it is a common size."

"Exactly," said Holmes. "And that is the point, but what if we were to try an experiment?"

Without waiting for an answer from Hopkins or anyone else, Holmes grabbed a pencil off of the desk. He turned the pencil at an oblique angle to the notepad, almost on its side. He carefully ran the pencil across the pad from side to side covering the sheet with markings from the lead. Gradually words began to appear in white amongst the black of the lead. The words were:

You can't save her. Anne Benton dies at five for her sins.

CHAPTER SIX

"*T*he words of the note, Holmes," I gasped. The importance of this clue was not lost upon me. "Then the note was written in this very house."

"So it would appear, Doctor."

"This is monstrous, Holmes," said I. "This means the killer was a person known to Miss Benton, and not simply a tramp or some such person."

"But we already knew that, Doctor."

"How, Holmes?"

"By the fact that it was delivered to the home of her landlord, and also the home, I might add, of the closest friends of the deceased and her brother."

"There is another possibility, Mr. Holmes, which I am certain you know very well," said Inspector Hopkins.

"Indeed I do, Hopkins. I am pleased to see that you are able to employ my methods, at least somewhat."

"Well, I know your methods as well, Holmes, and I am completely befuddled. Will you illuminate the situation for me, or am I to be left in the dark?"

I had spoken directly to my friend, but as his silence grew it was apparent to me, and everyone else in the room, that Holmes had no intention of enlightening me. I then turned my attention to the young Inspector. At length he broke the silence in the room.

"The other obvious conclusion, Dr. Watson, is that Mr. Harold Highlander himself wrote the note and only pretended that it was delivered to his house," said Hopkins grimly. "What have you to say to this, Mr. Highlander? This is damning evidence."

"Inspector, is a man in my position seriously to be suspected of murdering a young woman of whom I have a bare acquaintance?"

"It is a question that must be asked, sir," said Hopkins with some heat. "I must insist that you answer me."

"Very well then; consider it answered," said Highlander.

"I must insist upon a clear answer."

Highlander considered the words of the Inspector and finally decided that he had no other choice.

"If you insist, I deny writing the note," he said.

"It was delivered to me as I said. How could I have written it in any case? Miss Woodbury was with me the entire time."

"Come now, Mr. Highlander," said Hopkins. "You could have entered the house, written the note; and then gone back out and then made enough noise to draw Miss Woodbury from her house."

"At least you do not suspect me of the murder," huffed Highlander.

The expression on Hopkins's face told a different story, and Highlander noted it at once.

"So!" he cried. "You young pup, you will pay for such impertinence."

"All possibilities must be explored," said Hopkins. "A case can be made that you had opportunity. Motive is another question entirely, but that may take care of itself during the investigation."

"Mr. Holmes, I ask you directly," said Highlander. "As I said before, I know your reputation. I have listened to all that had been said, and I could not have committed the crime as it has been reckoned. Do you believe me guilty?"

Holmes had sat down behind the desk and was leaning backwards in the chair. His eyes were hooded and appeared almost shut. One unfamiliar with the detective might have supposed that he was sleeping, but I knew from long experience that this meant Holmes was in a state of great mental agitation. Seeing no response from his target, Highlander switched his attention back to the Inspector.

"Let me see if I understand your theory, Inspector Hopkins," he began in a lecturing tone. "According to your idea of the case, I murdered Miss Benton, for reasons unknown, and splattered her blood upon my shirt. I then burned the bloody and incriminating shirt, and took, I surmise, one of Mr. William Benton's shirts. Having accomplished this, I then wrote the note and went back outside. At this point I made certain that I am observed, and that Miss Woodbury would be able to attest that the lady was dead when I arrived. Am I fairly outlining your thinking in the matter?"

"That is one idea, Mr. Highlander," admitted Hopkins. "Mind you, it is only one idea. I have not said that you are a suspect, as of yet."

"Well, let me tell you that there is a difficulty with this scenario."

Highlander strode to the middle of the room and drew himself up to his full height, which was well over six feet tall. As he was so spare of frame, almost gaunt in fact, he appeared even taller.

"I admit that I do have an advantage on you, Inspector, and that is that I have met Mr. Benton. The brother of the deceased lady is every bit of six inches shorter in height than myself, and I would wager that he outweighs me by at least a stone. I could never have appropriated one of his shirts and hoped to pass it off as one of my own. Observe that my shirt is tailored specifically to my frame."

At his bidding everyone save Holmes leaned forward to examine the item in question. It was certainly a fine fit, and if Highlander was right about the build of Mr. Benton, then it did not seem likely that events could have played out as the Inspector had theorized.

"In addition," continued the man, "my suits are all from Savile Row in Mayfair. I doubt very much whether an ex-soldier such as Mr. Benton could afford such fine fare."

The statement was made with all the condescension common to the class of Harold Highlander, but the point was well taken. It was certainly hard to imagine the unseen invalided serviceman shopping the tony avenues in Mayfair for his apparel.

The Inspector was bloodied, but unbowed, and he seemed loath to relinquish his theory of the crime.

"Miss Woodbury, can you state with a certainty that Mr. Highlander did not enter the cottage before you became aware of his presence when he began pounding on the door?" he asked sharply.

No, I cannot, Inspector," she said, shooting a glance at Harold Highlander. "I was otherwise occupied and was not looking out the window. Besides which, it was already quite dark. I am not certain I would have noticed even had I been looking."

"A pity I was asleep," said Simon Langston suddenly and in a loud querulous voice. "I have mighty sharp eyes and darkness or no, I would have seen all. Me, a poor old man, with nothing better to do, I could have made this matter quite simple. At any rate, it is the height of foolishness to believe that a man of means such as Mr. Highlander could have been involved. He has a son and a family. That is something to live for. If my dear Jacob had lived, I would not be in the squalor that I find myself. He would have seen to it. And Miss Woodbury had a fine father as well. He was a good man and seeing the pain he was in at the end was awful. Lucky he had her, I say. If only I had been awake at my window!"

The old man had worked his way into a fever pitch and was breathing heavily.

"But you *were* asleep," said Hopkins. "Hopes

and prayers will not solve this crime."

"Aye, I was asleep," said the old man wistfully. "But if I had not been," he wagged a finger in the air, "I would bring this culprit to justice."

I smiled a bit at the injustice that the old man felt that had been done him by his inopportune afternoon nap. It was obvious he wished to play a part in the investigation. My experience has been that an elderly person in a neighborhood was often the biggest gossip of that neighborhood. I felt for the retired tailor's missed chance at a modicum of fame as the witness for the prosecution. As I finished musing about the elderly gentleman, I heard the voice of Sherlock Holmes.

"Miss Woodbury, how long have you resided in the cottage next door?" he asked.

"I grew up in the cottage, but I have been away for many years. I returned just over a year ago, Mr. Holmes," replied the startled woman.

"So, not that much longer, in fact, than the Bentons have lived here."

"That is so, Mr. Holmes. I had been away in Egypt most recently, and I returned when father wrote me of his illness."

"And you cared for him in his infirmity. May I ask

what was the illness that bedeviled him?"

"It was consumption, Mr. Holmes. It had spread throughout his lungs, and he had few days left by the time I managed to return."

"It is an ugly disease, my dear, and quite painful towards the end. Mr. Langston says he was in a great deal of pain."

"Oh, it was agony for him, Mr. Holmes. The doctors prescribed morphine, of course, but it could not halt the march of the disease itself."

"As I understand it those in close proximity to patients with consumption can be in danger of infection."

Holmes was right, of course, and many times such poor souls were isolated from others for just that reason. Miss Woodbury's father was fortunate to have a daughter to care for him.

"I cared not for the danger, sir," she said, with a sniffle and the hint of a tear, which she quickly dried. "I would have done anything for him."

"Of course, still I am surprised that you remain in the cottage. I would have thought that you would have resumed your travels after his death."

"I had planned to. I had never had to worry

about money, as father paid for my travels, you see. I had thought that he had a large nest egg built up, but I found when the estate was finally settled that little was left. As such my traveling days seemed at an end, at least temporarily; and here I remain."

"It must have been a shock for you to help find the body of a murder victim on this sleepy lane."

"As you say, it is not the type of place you should expect to find murder," she replied. "I can tell you in all candor that I was shocked to see poor Anne on the floor, stabbed as she was. It is hard for me to imagine how or why it was done."

I had noted a growing impatience from Inspector Hopkins as the elderly Simon Langston had rambled on. When Holmes himself seemed to career off onto a tangent as well, he became most anxious to bring the conversation back to the pressing topic of the unsolved murder.

"All of this is quite interesting, I am sure," he said. "I do not wish to hold anyone any longer than necessary and I believe that we have covered all the ground we can for this evening. Is there anything else from you, Mr. Holmes?"

"I have no more questions this night, Hopkins," said he.

"That is well," said Langston. "It is nearly time for bed for an old man such as myself."

Harold Highlander left with a bow to Holmes and myself. He pointedly ignored Hopkins, and walked out. Simon Langston followed on his heels, and Miss Woodbury was the last to leave, bidding us a gracious goodnight.

Hopkins made some notes for a minute or two before he addressed Holmes.

"What do you make of it, Mr. Holmes?" he asked. "I thought we were on the trail there for a moment. What is our next step?"

"My next step is to return to Baker Street," said Holmes. "I hope a sovereign was enough to hold the hansom."

"Baker Street!" cried Hopkins. "Do you mean to say you have given up?"

"Calm yourself, Hopkins," said Holmes with a smile. "We are not beaten, and I have given up nothing. We do, however, need to speak with the brother of the deceased and with the Highlander son, and his wife. For now we will put the assets of the Yard to good use. I ask that you have everyone's movements for today thoroughly examined."

"Of course, sir. And then?"

"Come see me at Baker Street tomorrow and I will outline our plan of advance; that is, pending new developments. Come, Watson, our carriage awaits."

CHAPTER SEVEN

*A*lthough Holmes and myself had settled on Baker Street by happenstance, the great detective would never entertain the idea of leaving for larger rooms for several reasons. Not the least of which were the cooking skills of our landlady, Mrs. Hudson. Though Holmes was not thought to be a man of tastes, at the breakfast board he was an admirer of the culinary arts of the lady in question and the beauty of her breakfast table.

The next morning found us enjoying the repast set on our sideboard. Holmes generally allowed no conversation of a case during his meals, and that day was no exception. My friend was expounding on the migratory patterns of passenger pigeons and the possible relationship of that pattern to the magnetic field of the planet. He further speculated that the clearing of wooded areas for cultivation of crops would lead to the extinction of the once-numerous bird. I was not, of course, an ornithologist, but I must admit that I doubted Holmes's theory of the demise of the species. As a young man I had read the writings and admired the paintings of Audubon. His descriptions of the immense flocks of these birds, some millions in composition, made a mass extinction in the near future seem very unlikely. However, Holmes was quite insistent that he would sadly be proven correct. He also made an observation about the role of passenger pigeon dung in promoting forest fires, which I found most inappropriate for the dining table.

As we moved to the sitting room for coffee and tobacco, I found my mind alive with the murder from the previous evening. Holmes was leaning back in his chair in his dressing gown and seemed oblivious to my preference in conversation. I decided that I would outwait the detective and force him to bring up the subject. Holmes liked to pretend that my curiosity was such that it did not allow me to reflect upon the evidence, but rather caused me to rush headlong into incorrect, and hasty, assumptions. I determined not to give him cause to further that theory, lit my own bowl of pipe weed and relaxed in my chair. After some time I noticed several sidelong glances from my friend. Following an hour-long silence, I was rewarded with the great man broaching the subject that was uppermost in my mind.

"You have been uncharacteristically reticent this day, Watson," he said, in a somewhat sullen manner. Holmes had become habituated to parceling out information on a case to me only at my pleadings. To my mind my small strike was already paying off dividends.

"I was reluctant to pursue the matter, as you seemed to have driven it from your mind," I said blandly. "It is perhaps the influence of Mycroft upon you."

"You feel that I have grown slothful, old friend?" Holmes mused.

"Perhaps not quite so far as slothful, but I cannot help but think that there have been occasions when you would have already dashed off several telegrams and even put the Irregulars to employment," said I.

"One must not mistake energy for execution, Doctor," he returned. "I simply await developments."

"You expect something of note to happen in the case?"

"Unless I am very much mistaken, something will happen today; tomorrow at the latest. At that point, I will be ready to proceed. Indeed, I am champing at the bit, appearances to the contrary notwithstanding."

As he finished his small speech, I saw the familiar fire in the eyes of the man. Holmes was not one to let grass grow beneath his feet; my small jibes at him aside. I wondered just what it was that he was expecting.

"Perhaps the brother has been found," I essayed. "If one of his shirts is missing, then we will know the gender of the culprit, at least."

"That is so," said he. "I am certain that Scotland Yard has employed their army of men in the effort to track Mr. Benton down. Though lacking somewhat in able men of detection, they have the numbers to search the whole of England. However, Watson, I believe that the quality race belongs to myself, with you included, of course."

I smiled at Holmes's inclusion of me in his compliment to himself, but in the main I was forced to agree with his assertion. The detectives of the Yard, though energetic, did not, save perhaps Gregson and Hopkins, employ the proven methods of Sherlock Holmes. Some of this refusal could be laid at the feet of institutional lethargy to embrace change. However, much, if not all of it, was in response to the small rivalry that was undoubtedly felt by the detectives of the Yard in relation to my friend. His every victory was a stab to the heart of that great English police force. Holmes himself largely deflected public credit for the cases he solved in conjunction with the Yard, but my published stories had created a much different picture that illuminated, correctly in my mind, the true nature of the collaboration.

"We have also yet to meet the son of Mr. Highlander and the son's wife," I reminded Holmes. "It is possible they can shed some light on this dark mystery."

"It is true that the cast is not yet complete, Doctor. However, I believe the development of which we await is now at hand. I hear footsteps upon the stairs. Will you attend at the door, please?"

I was no sooner out of my chair than the door was thrust open and our page admitted Inspector Hopkins. The Inspector was dressed nattily in a grey suit and hat. His eyes were bright and his manner betrayed an eagerness to share some new information. He greeted Holmes and myself and was quickly shown to a seat. He refused the offer of a cigarette or pipe from Holmes.

"Well, Hopkins, you are certainly out with the morning dew," stated Holmes. "Is there news you wish to share on the Benton case?"

"The case has been solved, sir," said Hopkins.

"Solved, you say. How has this been accomplished in so short a period of time?"

"A confession takes little time, sir," replied the Inspector.

"Indeed, so Harold Highlander has confessed," said Holmes calmly.

Hopkins nearly jumped from his seat and, I confess, I nearly came to my feet as well in surprise.

"How has this news reached you, Mr. Holmes?" asked the astonished man. "He walked into my office only one hour ago and turned himself in. Did he come here first? He made no mention of that fact."

"He made no mention of the fact because he did not come here first," said Holmes.

"I can attest to that, Inspector," said I. "Holmes and I have had no visitors this day save yourself. I must confess that I am much surprised, even if Holmes is not. Please, tell us all."

"Of course, Doctor," said Hopkins, as he regained both his composure and his good humour. "The tale is a simple one," he said, removing his notebook from his pocket for perusal. "Harold Highlander came into the Yard this morning and confessed that he had struck the lady with the candlestick in self-defense and she attacked him with the knife. In disarming her, he accidentally, according to his account, stabbed her in the chest, thus delivering the fatal blow."

"My word," said I. "So it was as simple as all that. This is a feather in your cap, surely, Hopkins."

"Not that there was much detective work, I am afraid," he observed wryly. "If only every criminal had the good manners to confess, then I might be home for my dinner on a more regular basis."

I laughed at the small joke of the man and noticed that Holmes did not join in the merriment.

"My only regret, of course, is pulling you into this, Mr. Holmes," he said. "Had I known the case was going to be this simple, I would not have bothered you. It was the note that threw me. It caused me to believe that the case was more complicated than it actually was."

Holmes merely waved a hand, but I rose to his defense.

"I say, Hopkins," I said with some heat. "Surely, Holmes played a role in this confession. It was he who demonstrated that the note was written in the cottage, and it was he who raised the question of why it was supposedly delivered to Harold Highlander in the first place. It must have been these points that drove Mr. Highlander to confess. Without Holmes, the case would still lie in darkness."

"I did not mean to minimize your part in this, sir," said Hopkins contritely. "As the good doctor says, you certainly played an important role. It is possible that I placed too much importance on Harold Highlander's word."

"How so?" I asked.

"Well, the gentleman says that the killing was an accident, but that he got the wind up and dreamed up the business of the note to throw off suspicion. He claims he regretted it almost immediately and, that upon reflection, he decided this morning to do the correct thing and confess."

"So it was a question of morals," I said.

"That's just it, Doctor," cried Hopkins. "He says he realized that by denying his own guilt, he was putting others in jeopardy."

"What of the buttons in the fireplace?" asked Holmes quietly.

"Highlander made no mention of that, Holmes," returned Hopkins. "I admit it is a loose end, but with his confession, it does not seem important."

"Has the brother been located? And what of the alibi of the son and the daughter-in-law? What of the evidence of the footprints? What of the candlestick?"

The rapid-fire questions had Hopkins at somewhat of a loss, and he stuttered as he replied to his mentor.

"Well, sir…you see…it is just that…none of that seemed necessary anymore. I do not understand, sir. We have our man. What is this talk of side issues?"

"As you find them superfluous, there is no need for further discussion of the matter," said Holmes briskly.

"I will admit I am disappointed in your lack of method, but that is as it is. Since the case is finished, I will bid you good day."

Hopkins's face fell as Holmes finished and I saw the hurt and befuddlement in his eyes. He looked to me as if pleading for an ally, but he found none in me. After several desultory attempts to apologize to Holmes, he finally exited our rooms. I heard his heavy footsteps upon the stairs and felt a slight bit of empathy for his obviously crushed spirits. I walked to the window facing the street and observed him coming onto the sidewalk. He called for no cab and began a solitary plod down the street. I returned to my chair and found Holmes puffing at his pipe in agitation.

A promising student," he muttered under his breath. "It is a pity, but the best lessons are often the ones that hurt the most. He will learn in time."

"It would appear that the Yard sees this matter as a closed one, Holmes," I said. "Do you have a plan of action as to how to proceed? It is obvious that you are not satisfied."

"My action will depend upon events, but fear not, Doctor; my waiting is at an end, for action I will take."

I was pleased to see that Holmes had regained his good spirits following the uncomfortable ending with

Hopkins. He went to his desk and dashed off several telegrams. I did not bother to ask for their contents. Any attempt would surely be futile. Holmes called for our page and gave him instructions to have them dispatched at once.

We sat in silence for several minutes. I had nearly decided that I would essay a few questions upon the case, when I heard a knock at the door. The page could not have returned by this time, and I was about to answer the knock myself when the door opened, and a man strode in. He was a gentleman of some fifty years and was dressed in the finery of the city. His clothes were almost those of a dandy, but I dare say they complimented him. He was over average height and clean-shaven. He carried his hat in his hand and looked from Holmes to myself. He settled his eyes finally upon my friend.

"Do I have the honor of addressing Mr. Sherlock Holmes?" he asked.

"I am Sherlock Holmes," he answered. "Allow me to introduce my companion, Dr. Watson."

"I am Samuel Johnson," he said, with a short bow. He returned his focus solely to Holmes. "Sir, I have been told you are the greatest detective in all of England. Is that correct?"

"That is a bit like asking the cook if the roast is

good, Mr. Johnson," said Holmes. "The answer is an easy one, but the truth is found only in the eating. Would you accept my mere word?"

"I thought that perhaps you could demonstrate your powers," said the man, as he pulled a revolver from inside his coat. He pointed it directly at Holmes. I saw that the hammer was down, but his finger was on the trigger. I was poised to throw myself upon him as his attention was all on my friend, but I feared the weapon may discharge anyway.

"What demonstration did you have in mind?" asked Holmes stifling a yawn.

"Just this, Mr. Holmes," he said. "What will happen if I pull this trigger?"

CHAPTER EIGHT

*H*olmes seemed blissfully unconcerned about the implied threat, but I felt as though my heart would leap from my chest.

My dear Mr. Johnson," said Holmes calmly. "Nothing will happen if you pull the trigger."

"The weapon is loaded, Mr. Holmes, I assure you," returned the man.

"Oh, I do not doubt that. An unloaded weapon would lessen the impact of the demonstration."

"Then why will nothing happen if I pull the trigger, sir?"

"Because you hold in your hands a Colt Dragoon Revolver," said Holmes. "An 1860 model unless I am very much mistaken. This weapon is a single action revolver and cannot be fired unless the hammer is pulled back to the locked position. The trigger merely releases the hammer to fall upon the firing pin. Pulling the trigger with the hammer down will result in a very unsatisfactory outcome, if you wish to do me bodily harm."

The man stood for a moment with the revolver still pointed towards Holmes, when he suddenly burst into laughter.

"You, are the very man for me, Mr. Holmes," he said with admiration. "Nerves of steel, and you most certainly have proven to my satisfaction that you are a great detective. Please, forgive my somewhat dramatic test of your powers."

I was not inclined to forgive this ungentlemanly display, but Holmes evinced no irritation and waved the man to a seat.

"And what may I do for you, Mr. Johnson? I cannot believe that the performance you have conducted was only for your amusement."

"Indeed it was not, Mr. Holmes," said the man heartily. "And Dr. Watson, I can see that you found the display distasteful. Perhaps it was, but I am in desperate straits, and I needed to know the measure of the man whom I ask for aid."

I nodded my head. I was still somewhat raw over the theatrics that the man had employed, but Holmes was in fine temperament, so I decided to acquiesce with him in conduct toward Mr. Johnson.

"Mr. Holmes, I come here today to speak with you on the matter of Harold Highlander. He has been arrested in the murder of a young woman leasing a cottage from him."

"I am aware of the matter, sir," replied Holmes.

"How is this?" Johnson asked, clearly taken aback.

Holmes quickly explained that he had been on the scene himself and knew the relevant facts of the case.

"What I do not know, Mr. Johnson, is why you are here and what your interest in the case is."

"That is easily answered, sir," responded Johnson. "I am a stockbroker, and I am an old friend of Harold's. Our families go back in association several generations. I received a note from the gentleman last evening, very late. It was a message written in, what seemed to me to be, great agitation. He said that he had killed the girl, and that he was going to confess to the crime."

"And this surprised you," said Holmes.

"In a word I was flabbergasted, sir," said Johnson. "Mr. Holmes, I have known the man my entire life. It is beyond comprehension that he would take a life."

"Do you know the details of the crime?" asked my friend.

"The penny press is efficient, if not genteel," said Johnson with a grimace. "I have read all that has made it into print and I am even more convinced than ever that something is amiss."

"Why have the details caused you to further doubt the confession?"

"Simply because Harold is incapable of such violence. The very idea that he could bludgeon and stab a defenseless woman in cold blood is ludicrous."

"Men do many things of which they are not thought capable, Mr. Johnson, in cold blood," observed Holmes sagely. "Dr. Watson and I have seen many such examples of the degradation of the human animal from formerly pious and moral men, but from my understanding, the confession is one of the nature of a crime committed in hot blood."

"Is the difference that great?" asked Samuel Johnson.

"In execution perhaps not; but in planning, most certainly," said Holmes.

"Holmes," I cried. "Do you mean to imply that

the crime was one of premeditation made to appear as if it were committed in the heat of the moment?"

"Or perhaps the other way around, Doctor. I only make the point that Harold Highlander claims the crime was one of hot blood. In doing so it may be claimed by the police, and the courts, that previous behavior is not indicative in this matter. In other words, though a gentle man may not plan a murder, such a man may strike out violently if in danger, or even if he senses danger. The fight or flight pattern is well established within the animal kingdom."

I was not certain that observations of wild animals were predictive upon human beings, but I did not argue the overall point, which, I did not doubt, was sound.

"In any event, as a friend of the man, you would testify to his gentle nature and his inability to be hard, or even ruthless, when necessary," said Holmes.

"I see your trap there, Mr. Holmes, and I am certain that in business Harold has made many a decision that weighed against the other man," said he. "I admit that in matters of money he could be a harsh and flinty opponent, but he was a dedicated family man and a true gentleman. He was completely devoted to his late wife, and, though he had no daughters, I simply cannot see him striking down a woman of age to have been his daughter."

I could see that Holmes was weighing the words of Johnson. I could see nothing in his story other than that of a devoted friend trying to help another friend in a time of great need.

"I take it that you are acquainted with the son and the son's wife, Mr. Johnson."

"Of course," replied he. "David and Sylvia are friends as well. We do not run in the same circles of society, but I count them as dear friends nevertheless."

"What does Mr. David Highlander do for a living, if anything?" asked Holmes.

"He sees to the family shipping concerns."

"Then the senior Highlander is a man of retirement."

"Yes, in the main, but it is a titular position really. The company board runs the business, with David as a mere figurehead, which suits him very well. David is a man interested in cards and horses above all else. A day riding and an evening of bridge is his idea of Eden."

"And the wife?"

"Sylvia runs the household in the absence of Harold's wife. They have a devoted staff and when not at that, I assume she is much like every other woman of means. To my knowledge, she spends most of her afternoons, and a good deal of the Highlander money, in the shops of London."

"Have you, yourself, ever met the deceased, Mr. Johnson?"

"I have never seen the lady in life or in death."

"What of the brother, Mr. William Benton?"

"I have never met the man."

"What of the neighbors? Do you know Mr. Simon Langston?"

"I am not acquainted with him either, but I have heard the name. He was a tailor of some note when I was young. I have heard that he has had some financial setbacks in his declining years."

"Do you know Miss Elizabeth Woodbury?"

"Yes, but chiefly through her father. I was his stockbroker. I am Harold Highlander's broker as well. I had the occasion to meet Miss Woodbury when her father passed. She was his sole beneficiary, and his stocks were duly transferred to her. A very tidy sum, I might add."

"Do you remain her broker?"

"I am afraid she changed houses immediately upon the transfer. That is not unusual, and should not be taken as a indication of unhappiness with my firm."

Johnson made his last statement with some vigor. I wondered if he was unsettled by rumours of malfeasance and was thus sensitive to the implication.

"I believe that I have a full grasp of your relationship to those involved, Mr. Johnson, but one item remains."

"What is that, Mr. Holmes?"

"Just what is it that you expect me to do, sir?"

"Why, clear the name of a man falsely accused, of course," cried Johnson, nearly rising from his seat.

"Mr. Highlander does not stand accused, falsely or otherwise, sir," explained Holmes patiently. "He has confessed. Inspector Hopkins was here this very morning. Scotland Yard is satisfied of his guilt. As long as Harold Highlander professes his culpability, I see little that can be done."

Johnson was running his fingers through his hair, as does one in great agitation of mind.

"But do you not see, Mr. Holmes, that he must be in the throes of a sort of madness? Are you yourself satisfied with the explanation he has given? You were on the scene, as you say. Is the great Sherlock Holmes satisfied?"

Holmes did not reply at once, but he rose to his feet and crossed over to the unlit fireplace. He turned his back to us, and Samuel Johnson looked to me for guidance. Before I could respond, Holmes spoke.

"I am not satisfied, Mr. Johnson," he said. "I am not satisfied in the least."

CHAPTER NINE

A smile of satisfaction crossed the face of Samuel Johnson.

"So you will take the case, Mr. Holmes?" he asked hopefully. "I can assure you a handsome sum as a retainer and a generous fee upon completion. What is your first move?"

"I have already undertaken the first move before you arrived, Mr. Johnson," said Holmes with a smile.

Johnson plainly showed his surprise.

"Yes, it is true," said Holmes. "I am afraid that any reluctance on my part that you observed was in part an affectation. It was your intentions that I wished to be assured of. Now that I am, we can begin."

As Holmes was speaking, I heard the bell from the downstairs entrance. Within a matter of moments the door was opened by our page, who had apparently returned from his errand, and he ushered in three people, all of whom were unknown to me.

"Ah," cried Holmes. "Mr. Johnson, I believe we are about to meet some of the players we have been discussing."

In the lead of the small group were a man and a woman who were, obviously, man and wife. The one bringing up the rear, with his hat in hand, was a very dark man, solidly built, and of middle height. The man in the lead strode forward.

"Samuel, I hardly expected to find you here," he said. "Though I gather we are on similar errands."

"I suspect we are," said Johnson. "Mr. Holmes, allow me to introduce David Highlander and his wife, Sylvia Highlander."

Holmes nodded at both without rising. David Highlander bore a certain degree of resemblance to his father, as a son naturally would, but was shorter and stouter. He seemed somewhat ill at ease, but that was not surprising. Many people seeking the aid of Sherlock Holmes walked through the door with the same manner. His wife, Sylvia, was a handsome woman with dark hair. She was dressed in the fashion of the day, and she carried herself with confidence.

"And would this other gentleman be Mr. William Benton?" he asked.

"Indeed I am, sir," replied the man. "It was my

poor sister who was murdered. How could such a thing happen?"

"That is what we are here to discuss with Mr. Holmes," said the lady sharply.

"Of course, Sylvia," replied Benton. "But it is my sister who has been killed."

"Yes, and my father stands accused," said David Highlander. "I believe it shall drive me mad."

The man fell into a bit of a swoon, and he collapsed on our sofa. I realized that his uneasy manner had hidden great emotional distress just under the surface. His wife sat primly by him and waited for him to gain control of himself.

"Mr. Highlander, if you have come to engage my services, I fear that Mr. Johnson has already become my client," said Holmes.

David Highlander looked at Holmes, and then to Samuel Johnson with a vague expression of alarm.

"Samuel, you do not believe that father has committed this foul crime, do you?" he cried.

"Of course not," replied the suave financier. "I have already explained to Mr. Holmes that your father has lost his senses, at least temporarily."

"That is certainly the case," said Mrs. Highlander. "Even William does not believe it, and as he has said, he is an aggrieved party."

"Is that so, Mr. Benton?" prodded Holmes.

"It is, Mr. Holmes," said the dark man. "I cannot see Mr. Highlander bludgeoning and stabbing poor Anne."

At the mention of the bloody crime scene, Sylvia Highlander's flinty reserve broke. Tears sprang into her eyes, and I feared the lady would have a spell as her husband had. I reached for my handkerchief, but I was beaten to the punch by William Benton, who pulled his own from his jacket pocket and handed it to the lady. She accepted with thanks, and dabbed at her eyes with the borrowed piece of cloth.

I noted at once that Holmes had observed the exchange very closely. It occurred to me that he had thought that, perhaps the lady's grief had been feigned. Her response had seemed quite genuine to me, but if Holmes discerned something more he was keeping his own counsel as usual.

"You are late of the army?" asked Holmes of William Benton.

It seemed that the lady's display of emotion was not going to deter my friend from the investigation, as he quickly put the focus back upon the question at hand.

"That is so, Mr. Holmes."

"Your family has a long military history, does it not, Mr. Highlander?" asked Holmes.

"No, Mr. Holmes," said David Highlander in some confusion.

"Now, surely I have heard differently," said Holmes. "I had thought that the Highlanders had served the crown for generations."

"There may have been the odd member of the family in the military, Mr. Holmes, but there is no family tradition."

Holmes lit a pipe and remained silent for a minute. He finally looked up and returned his attention to William Benton.

"I have heard that you were in India," Holmes said.

"I have only returned in the past six months, sir."

"Do you have any relations in England?"

"Anne was all I had left, sir," he replied, and this time I thought I detected tears in his eyes.

"What of friends?" asked Holmes.

"None, save the two in this room, of course," said Benton. "I'm afraid all my chums are still on the subcontinent."

"I see," said Holmes. "And your sister, likewise, was largely alone in England?"

"That is so."

"That is odd."

"Why is that odd, Mr. Holmes?" asked Johnson.

"Only that someone knew the lady well enough to have a motive to kill her, and yet her circle of friends and acquaintances was seemingly quite small," said Holmes.

"You think that I may have been the target, Mr. Holmes?" asked a perplexed William Benton.

"It is possible," replied Holmes. "But we have the same difficulty. You are quite alone as well."

Holmes's logic was, as always, unassailable. I saw concerned expressions of the faces of all in the room, save Mrs. Highlander. Her expression was one of exasperation. She finally could contain herself no longer.

"Then perhaps it was just some tramp, or

common burglar," she burst out. "It has always seemed to be the most likely explanation to me."

"That simply cannot be the solution, Mrs. Highlander," said Holmes calmly.

"And why not?" challenged the lady. "It seems to me that you men are making a mystery here where none really exists."

"Calm yourself, Sylvia," David Highlander pleaded.

"The lady asks a direct question, and it deserves a direct answer," said Holmes. "The note threatening the life of Miss Benton precludes the idea that this was a murder by someone not acquainted with the lady. Whether Harold Highlander wrote the note himself, as he now claims, or someone else wrote it, the idea of a passing stranger as a perpetrator is not defensible."

Mrs. Highlander had listened patiently to the words of Sherlock Holmes. At his conclusion she appeared to be on the verge of gainsaying him, but something stayed her hand and she remained silent.

"Then what is the next course of action, Mr. Holmes?" asked Samuel Johnson. "I believe I can speak for the group when I say that we are in your hands."

I saw nods from those assembled at the

statement from the stockbroker.

"As uncomfortable as it may be," began Holmes, "we must eliminate Miss Benton's known associates from consideration. I will need to know where each of you were during the crucial time in question."

"Do you mean we are to be suspected?" asked Sylvia Highlander. "Why, what motive would any of us have for such a foul crime?"

"Let us leave motive aside for now," said Holmes. "For the moment, let us see if we can eliminate each of you simply by lack of opportunity."

"But, Mr. Holmes, the police have not questioned us about our movements. If they do not suspect us, why should you?" asked Harold Highlander.

"Mr. Highlander, the police have dropped the investigation in its entirety because of the confession of your father," said Holmes with a sigh. "They believe that the case is at an end. If you do as well, I suggest that you come to terms with your father's imprisonment or execution."

David Highlander pulled a handkerchief from his jacket pocket and mopped his brow with it. He replaced it and met the gaze of Sherlock Holmes.

"Of course, you are right, Mr. Holmes," he said

in a firm voice. "As for myself, I can tell you that I went riding yesterday afternoon at about two o'clock and came home shortly after five. Finding the house empty, I returned to the stables to see to my horse. He had come up slightly lame during our ride, and I went back to the house after seven to find my wife there and my father still out. Of course, we had no idea where he was until later that night."

"Did anyone ride with you?" asked Holmes.

"No, I rode alone that day," he said slowly. "But people must have seen me. I often go riding, as anyone could tell you."

"Of course," said Holmes. "Now, Mrs. Highlander, would you be so kind as to describe your movements."

"Certainly, Mr. Holmes, if it will help to set you on the correct path, we can at least eliminate me," she said haughtily. "I went shopping early in the afternoon. I should say that it was about one o'clock, and I returned well after six. I was in West End shops in which I am well known. There can be no question that I was well away from the area when poor Anne was murdered."

At the mention of the killing, I saw both David Highlander and William Benton visibly wince.

"And you, Mr. Benton," asked Holmes, switching

his attention to the dark, swarthy ex-soldier.

"I was in Kent for the past two days, sir, looking for work as an estate manager," he said. "I stayed last evening at the Red Lion. I had dinner at the inn and retired early. Just after seven, I should say. I returned this morning to the awful news."

"I see. And had you ever seen your sister wearing the black top she was found in?"

"I do not believe so, sir. I believe it was part of a mourning dress."

"Quite likely," responded Holmes.

Holmes was taking no notes, but I was writing down the whereabouts of the group should he need them later. Everyone had told his or her story in a straightforward manner, and I had detected no evasion. If the alibis were not airtight in all cases, it was really no surprise. Most people could not be called upon to account for every minute of a day, but when murder had been done that was another matter. Holmes, after some silent reflection, turned his attention to Samuel Johnson.

"And what of your movements, Mr. Johnson?" he asked.

"My movements? But, Mr. Holmes, I came to hire you today," he said with amusement. "Surely I would not be attempting to prove the innocence of my friend if I were the culprit. What motive would I have for doing such a thing?"

"As I said before," replied my friend, "we are putting aside the issue of motive, and that includes why a guilty man might engage my services. For now, I must insist upon a statement of your movements yesterday afternoon."

Johnson studied Holmes for some moments. His face was clouded with anger, I thought, but it gradually softened until the man broke into a smile, and then into laughter.

"Very well, Mr. Holmes," he said with some mirth. "I am the top man in my field and I am not accustomed to following orders, but then again, you are the top man in your field. Very well. I left the firm at noon yesterday to dine in my home as I always do. I did not return, as I was studying a prospectus of a Brazilian rubber plantation, which I was considering recommending to my clients. I was alone all afternoon and saw no one until I received Harold's note late last night."

"You reside nearby to the Highlander home?"

"I do, Mr. Holmes. Only a short walk away. Less than one-half mile."

"So, in fact, you live quite close to the murder scene as well."

Holmes stated it as a fact, rather than a question and Johnson merely nodded in the affirmative.

"I can assure you all," Holmes continued, "that if the case against Mr. Harold Highlander falters, your movements will come under the microscope of the Yard. I myself may lack the resources to question every shopkeeper in the West End, the inns of Kent, or those who might have observed Mr. Highlander on his ride, but the police do have the resources. What they lack in detective skills, they make up for in energy. Of this, I assure you. Has each of you told the truth to me? Even the smallest evasion will be looked upon as evidence of guilt, if uncovered later."

The three men of the group were nodding in agreement with Holmes's statement, but I noticed that the lips of Sylvia Highlander were pursed in apparent disapproval. I watched her as her expression passed mere disapproval, and moved into open agitation. Finally, she could contain herself no further and she burst out.

"David, can you not see that you will not be able to maintain this pretense any longer?" she shrieked.

CHAPTER TEN

*D*avid Highlander was in shocked silence for a moment and then replied to his wife in anger.

"Sylvia, shut up!" he said savagely. "You do not know what you are saying!"

The husband glared at his wife for some moments, but she would not be cowed and stuck her chin out defiantly.

"Mrs. Highlander, do you dispute your husband's accounting of his whereabouts?" asked Holmes in an even tone of voice.

David Highlander looked petulantly at his wife, but she was nodding her head as Holmes spoke.

"I do, Mr. Holmes. David has told a stupid lie out of vanity. I have let him maintain this fiction so as not to embarrass him, but your admonition of giving a false alibi has moved me to speak."

"What is the true story then, madam?" asked Holmes.

"David did go riding earlier in the day as he said, but when I returned home he was not in the stables. I found him insensible with drink and asleep in his bedchamber. His compulsion for strong drink has grown in recent years and the state in which I discovered him is one in which I am very familiar. I blame his father for this weakness manifesting itself in David. His father has given him no real authority over the shipping line and he consequently has far too much time on his hands. It has led him astray."

The truth of the lady's statement was read easily on the face of David Highlander. I recalled the words of Samuel Johnson. He had said that David Highlander was a mere figurehead at his father's firm. I had thought that perhaps the lack of responsibility was congenial to the man, but it would seem that it had weighed heavily upon him, and he had turned to drink for comfort.

"Will you give us a true accounting now, sir?" asked my friend. "You make my task more difficult with evasions, no matter what the reason."

David Highlander shifted uncomfortably in his seat and stared at the floor. With little emotion he replied to Holmes, "The first part of my story was true. I did go riding at two and I returned after five. Father was not about and I felt a chill. I admit that I had several toddies and fell asleep. I was certainly not overcome with drink, though. I am sorry that I held back that part of my story, but whether I was in the stables or in my room seems to matter little. In either case, I was not at the Benton cottage writing a note or killing poor Anne."

"David, buck up, my boy," said Johnson cheerfully. "No one suspects you, but Mr. Holmes is correct. Only the truth will free your father."

David Highlander nodded his head absentmindedly as the stockbroker spoke. His wife sat with her lips pursed and her hands on her lap. William Benton was smoking a cigarette and seemed lost in thoughts of his own.

"Well, let us move on to Mr. Harold Highlander's movements," said Holmes. "When he left the Benton cottage I assume he went directly home. Is that true, Mr. Highlander?"

"What's that, Mr. Holmes?" asked the young man. "Oh, yes. Father returned home at around eight. He gave us the terrible news. I was in the drawing room by that time and he joined me. We were all in shock, I assure you. I was stunned to hear that Anne had been stabbed to death. Even now it is hard to believe."

"Were you all together to hear your father's tale?"

"I was in the kitchen attending to dinner with

the cook," said Sylvia Highlander. "I heard the front door open, and I joined David and his father. They were already discussing the matter when I arrived. My father-in-law told us the terrible story and then retired to his study and I saw him no more that night."

"Did he give any indication of his plans to confess?"

"None," replied David. "He was upset, of course, but he certainly did not intimate that he planned this mad scheme of confessing to the murder."

"So after Mr. Highlander retired to his study, he was seen no more by anyone until this morning?" asked Holmes.

"He was seen, Mr. Holmes," stated David Highlander.

"By whom, sir?"

"James, the butler, told me this morning that Simon Langston came by quite late and met with father in his study."

"That horrid little tailor," exclaimed Sylvia Highlander in disgust. "Why would he come to see your father?"

"I cannot say," replied her husband. "James says that Langston claimed that father had sent for him. At any rate he says that father received the man. They met for nearly half an hour and James saw the man out."

"How extraordinary," I exclaimed. "What can it mean, Holmes?"

"There are two men that know the answer to that, Doctor," said he. "I assure you, that the question will be put to both of them. It is not, perhaps, a completely unexpected development."

"Then you see some daylight in this matter," said Johnson.

"Perhaps," said Holmes in return, "but much work remains to be done."

"Still, your words give me hope," said the tall stockbroker.

"You speak for me, Samuel," cried David Highlander. "For the first time today I dare dream of an escape from this nightmare. Isn't this marvelous, Sylvia?"

"Nothing has been accomplished yet, David," the woman stated bluntly. "Mr. Holmes has given us mere words. I would remind you that things still look very black."

David Highlander seemed to physically shrink as his wife spoke.

"Of course, my dear," he said in a low voice. He turned to Holmes. "Still, we are in your hands, Mr. Holmes. What else can we tell you?"

"I believe that I have all that I need at this moment in order to begin," said Holmes. "I will be in touch with each of you. Good day."

At the abrupt dismissal, I saw stunned faces. Samuel Johnson and Sylvia Highlander were both insistent on hearing Holmes's next step, but he refused to be moved to further conversation. After several minutes of pleading, the room was finally cleared of our guests. Holmes resumed his seat and began puffing on his pipe. I likewise returned to my chair and waited for the great detective's next move. I had been surprised by Holmes's decision to halt any further questioning of the guests, but I had learned from long experience to trust the judgment of Sherlock Holmes. After some ten minutes of attention to his pipe, Holmes turned and addressed me.

"I see that you are in agreement with our client and the lady, Doctor," he said. "No, no. Do not deny it. I read the disapproval on your face."

"It is not disapproval, Holmes," I protested. "It is merely surprise. Surely the time to question these people was here and now."

"We have their stories, Watson. Whether they

are true or not, we will not discover without effort. This crime will not be solved from this flat, I assure you."

"Then you have a plan, Holmes?" I asked eagerly. "How will we proceed?"

"We have already started, Doctor. The cables I sent out this morning will answer several questions I have. In addition there is work yet to be done today here in London."

"That is more in line with my thinking. Where away are we?"

"I am afraid it is not we this time, Watson." I fear that I showed my disappointment too clearly. "I am sorry, old friend; I must conduct this part of our investigation alone, but you do have a role to play."

"I suppose that I am to stay here and await messages," I said somewhat glumly. "Really, Holmes, I am more than your secretary."

"Doctor, I assure you that I value your skills. Indeed you have an important role in the investigation."

"And what is that, Holmes?" I asked suspiciously.

Instead of answering, Holmes swept from the room into his bedchamber. When he did not return immediately, I began to pace the floor. To be kept in the dark was business as usual with Holmes, but I still felt aggrieved at times in my association with the great detective. As I was nursing my perceived slights, Holmes returned to the sitting room. He had changed from his normal clothing into the uniform of a livery driver.

"Are you changing professions, Holmes?"

"That is actually very droll, Doctor," he replied. "I must mix among the working classes today, and this uniform is the perfect costume in which to make my way in that world."

"I take it you wish to speak to the stable boys, delivery men, servants and the like in the area of the crime."

"Very perceptive, Doctor."

"But surely, Holmes, the police have already covered that ground."

"Perhaps, but remember the Yard believes the case to be solved. They are likely not asking any more questions, unless Hopkins has had a change of heart. In any case, many mouths close when a policeman is the questioner and not a fellow workman buying a drink. People often do not like to speak to a officer of the law asking questions, but will revel in gossip with a bar mate."

"But is there any value in mere gossip, Holmes?"

Holmes laughed a throaty laugh, and I noticed that his entire posture was different from the norm. Instead of the ramrod straight bearing of my friend, I saw a slightly slouching roustabout. Holmes mastered his mirth and continued.

"There are no secrets of the upper class from the servant and working classes, I assure you, Watson. I hope to find much information that will aid us in our quest."

"In that case, I ask again. What am I to do in your absence?"

"I wish for you to visit Mr. Langston and Miss Woodbury. I would like your general impressions of them and I would ask that you report to me what type of teapot they each possess."

"Teapot? What in the world do teapots have to do with this mystery? Are you jesting with me, Holmes?"

"I assure you, Doctor, I am in earnest."

"But how I am to do this without causing comment?"

"My dear doctor, it is really quite simple. You do yourself an injustice by speaking without thinking."

I furrowed my brow in concentration, and then it came to me.

"I suppose I could simply arrive at tea time. Is that what you suggest, Holmes?"

"Precisely, Watson. You know, you are really coming along quite nicely."

CHAPTER ELEVEN

I gave Holmes a wry smile at his jab.

"Do you wish for me to visit these people in any particular order?" I asked.

"I should think that it would be well that you call upon Mr. Langston first."

"What shall I say if they ask me about the state of the investigation?"

"You may tell them that I have been engaged to uncover the true culprit of the crime. In fact, that is the other reason I wish you to go. I want the news of the investigation well known. But remember, I wish you to employ your judgment and simply engage these two in conversation."

"While everyone's eye is upon me, you will be free to make your own inquiries."

Just so, Watson," said he. "I am off. I will likely be quite late, Watson, so do not await my return. I shall surely see you in the morning."

With those words Holmes slouched from the rooms. I spent the next several hours in contemplation. Holmes obviously had a theory as to the identity of the murderer, but I could see nothing save for the fact that Harold Highlander had confessed to the crime. When I had judged that the time was right, I departed our rooms and engaged a hansom for the ride to Lambs Lane.

The trip was without event and I soon found myself in front of the dilapidated cottage of Simon Langston. I did not ask the carriage to await me, as I knew not how long my task would take. I walked to the front door of the home and knocked briskly. The door was opened rather quickly, and I saw a look of definite surprise upon the face of Simon Langston.

"Why, it is Doctor Watson," he exclaimed. "You do my poor house honor, sir. Please come in. I was just about to sit down to tea. Will you join me?"

I was overjoyed that Holmes's plan had worked out so well, and I eagerly assented to the old man's invitation. Langston led me into a small sitting room that nearly matched the outside of the home in shabbiness. It was clean, but it was obvious that the roof was leaking, as there were water stains on the walls and ceiling. Langston evinced no embarrassment at the state of the room. Taking my cue from him, I sat in a chair by the fireplace. The table between us held two cups and the pot, and my host poured me a cup of tea and then one for himself.

As Holmes had instructed me to observe the teapot, I did so closely. It seemed a common piece of earthenware and was noticeably chipped.

"Well, Doctor," said Langston, "I see that Mr. Holmes is not satisfied with events."

"What do you mean, Mr. Langston?"

"There is no need to be coy with me, sir. I have spoken with Mr. Benton this day, and he told me of his visit to your rooms. I had thought the matter was settled."

The thought of an active investigation seemed to energize the elderly man. He leaned forward as he spoke.

"It is true that Holmes had agreed to look into the matter further, but I fear I am not in his confidence. Have you any ideas on the case?"

"Me?" he asked with a grin. "I am a simple tailor, Doctor. I have no head for solving crimes. I will leave that for the young people. I am content to merely survive in my small home."

I glanced around the room and again noted the dilapidated appearance of the house. I caught Langston watching me, and he broke into a broad grin once more.

"Oh, I know this place needs some repairs, but I may be moving soon."

"Indeed, Mr. Langston. Where might you be going?"

"Not far, Doctor. In fact, to tell a secret, I will be moving into the Benton cottage soon. It is in a much better state than this one. I have already discussed it with Mr. Highlander."

"I would have thought that David Highlander would be worried about other matters than the cottage," I said.

"It was Mr. Harold Highlander, Doctor. He sent for me last night. He said the Benton lease was up soon and that he would not renew it given the circumstances. That being the case, he offered it to me."

So that explained the visit to the Highlander home last night, I thought.

"Of course, I had no idea that the gentleman was going to confess to murder the next morning," Langston continued. "At any rate, I will be more comfortable than I am here. That is certain."

"But this will be an additional blow to William Benton. First his sister is murdered, and now he will lose his home. That seems rather hard on him."

"I have already talked to Mr. Benton this day. He is anxious to move on as well. He tells me that he has a job offer in Kent and plans to leave soon. The boy does not strike me as the type to stay for long in any one place."

"Soldiers are often like that, Mr. Langston," said I.

"As you say, Doctor."

I finished my tea and talked for some time more with the tailor, but he seemed to grow weary as we spoke and I finally arose and took my leave. I bade the old man to stay seated and saw myself out. As I was walking down the path towards the lane, I observed William Benton likewise leaving his home, carrying a small case. He gave me a friendly wave, and we met at his gate.

"I did not expect to see you so soon, Doctor," he said in a casual manner.

"I was just making a friendly call on Mr. Langston. I understand that you have obtained work."

"It did not take long for word to spread, I see," Benton said. "I take it that our town crier has been the source of your news."

He gestured towards the Langston place as he

spoke. I acknowledged that Simon Langston had told me of his new employment.

"Nothing much gets by the old crow, I suppose," he said, with an undertone of slight rancor. "But that is neither here nor there, I suppose."

"Did you discover if any of your shirts are missing, Mr. Benton?"

"Ah, yes, the missing shirt. David explained that theory. None of mine are missing, but I really could not say if any of poor Anne's are not there. She had many outfits, and you know what women are, Doctor. You must excuse me now. I have several telegrams I need to send out. The nearest office is just down the lane."

We parted and I watched as he quickly walked away with his head bowed. I noticed a carriage was in front of Miss Woodbury's cottage. It had certainly not been there when I had arrived earlier, and I wondered who was calling upon the lady. Holmes had told me to use my own judgment, so I decided to make my visit to Miss Woodbury, regardless of her guest. I knocked at her door and was cheerfully received by the lady herself.

"Why, Dr. Watson, please come in and join us," she said with a smile.

I followed her into the sitting room of the cottage and found that her visitor was Sylvia Highlander.

"Hello again, Doctor," she said. "I came to see Elizabeth and invited myself to tea. I practically forced the poor girl to brew up a pot. Isn't that right, Elizabeth?"

"Now, Sylvia, you will make Dr. Watson think I am not a proper host. Please, sit down, Doctor, and let me pour you a cup."

I did as I was bid, and soon found myself with a cup of tea in one hand and a biscuit in the other. Sylvia Highlander was chattering away, and I used the opportunity to study the teapot of Elizabeth Woodbury. It was much more delicate and exotic than the one I had seen in Simon Langston's home. There were curious drawings on the pot and I wondered where it had come from. I decided to take the direct approach.

"I say, Miss Woodbury, this is an unusual teapot. Where did you find it? Surely it is not of English manufacture."

"Indeed not, Doctor," replied the lady. "I found that in a marketplace in Egypt. They are made by the natives, and they say the process has not changed for a thousand years, but that may just be a tale. I am not an antiquities expert."

"The Doctor speaks for me, Elizabeth," said Sylvia Highlander. "I think it is most unusual as well. May I see it?"

Miss Woodbury handed the pot to her guest who examined it closely.

It really is most exotic," said Miss Highlander. "How I envy your travels. I have never been able to pry David from England."

"Well, my travels seem to be at an end as well, Sylvia. England, dreary as it is at times, is my home and I am content."

"That is well said, Elizabeth. David would certainly endorse that view."

Sylvia Highlander began to hand the pot back to Miss Woodbury, when it slipped from her hands and crashed to the floor of the cottage.

"Oh dear," exclaimed Mrs. Highlander. "Elizabeth, how clumsy of me. I am so sorry."

"Think nothing of it, Sylvia," said the lady, as she knelt and began to pick up the broken shards. "It was a mere curio and of no real value."

The lady seemed sincere in her acceptance of the apology, and she excused herself from the room to clear away the remains of the pot. I took advantage of her absence to question Sylvia Highlander.

"I was not aware that you and Miss Woodbury were social friends," I said.

"We do not generally make calls on one another, Doctor, but these are not normal times. I wanted to make certain that Elizabeth was all right. She is quite alone in the world, you know."

My reply was interrupted by the reappearance of our host. Sylvia Highlander took that moment to announce that she had to return home. She left, and I heard her carriage clatter down the lane. I listened until the noise faded completely away.

"Does Mr. Holmes believe that Mr. Highlander is innocent?" Elizabeth asked. "Sylvia told me that he had agreed to look into the case for David."

"Actually, Mr. Samuel Johnson is Holmes's client," I replied. "But I am afraid that I am overstaying my welcome. After all, I am an uninvited guest. I only wanted to see if you were all right. You have had quite a jolt."

"That is true, Doctor. I thank you for coming by."

She arose and walked me to the door. As she opened it, I saw that dusk was beginning. I felt a shiver come over me.

"It gets dark quite early this time of year," she observed.

I agreed and took my leave of her. I walked to

the lane and began to trudge back towards the center of the great city. I felt no happiness at the thought of the weary journey I could be in for before I might be able to engage a hansom. As I walked I thought of the murdered girl and wondered if Holmes had made any progress. I was deep in thought when I realized a carriage was coming up behind me. It halted next to me, and the driver leaned over from his seat.

"Would you be needing a carriage, guv'nor?" he asked in a reedy voice.

"I would, and you're a godsend, my boy," I replied, and climbed into the cab. I gave the driver the address of 221B Baker Street and settled in for the unexpected ride. I was nearly asleep, although the night was still young, when the cab jolted to a halt and I realized I was home. I climbed from the cab and offered the driver a sovereign. I was almost to the front door when I heard the voice of Sherlock Holmes.

"Am I to keep the change, Doctor? That is most generous."

I turned and saw that Holmes had been my driver and I had not realized it.

CHAPTER TWELVE

*M*y head was swimming at the sight of my friend grinning from atop his seat.

"Holmes, I will never understand your childish delight in fooling me, your faithful friend and companion."

"My apologies, Doctor, but I did save you a tiresome walk. Does that not earn a reprieve from your wrath?"

He had such a broad, friendly smile on his face that I felt my anger quite drain away.

"I do thank you for that, of course, Holmes, but was it necessary to maintain the pretense the entire ride home?"

"You never know who might be watching, Watson. My day is not done and it would not do for anyone to pierce my disguise before I have finished my investigation."

"Then it nears an end?" I asked.

"The last pieces of the puzzle are falling in place, Doctor. I have known since yesterday who the killer is, but I could not answer all the questions. By tomorrow all will be known."

"But, Holmes, you have not heard my report."

I quickly related all that I had seen and heard. I gave careful testimony as to the teapots and most especially the breaking of Miss Woodbury's pot by Mrs. Highlander. Holmes listened without asking questions until I finished my tale.

"You have done well, Doctor, and you have answered another question for me. It progresses, my friend."

"But what of the broken pot, Holmes? Does that upset your plans?"

Not at all, Doctor. Please think nothing else of it."

"But, why would Mrs. Highlander break it?"

"Did it seem to you that she broke the pot on purpose?"

"Well, no," I said hesitantly. "But it does seem to be quite a coincidence."

"That I will allow you, Doctor. It is an interesting

coincidence, but then, coincidences do happen. Did you observe the telegrams that William Benton wished to send?"

"No, but he had a small case with him. Any paper work was likely in there."

"Quite likely, Watson. There are many moving parts in the case."

"What of Langston's explanation for his visit to Harold Highlander?"

"We shall have to take his explanation at its own worth for now. As I understand it, Harold Highlander is answering no questions at this time. I will know all before dawn breaks again."

"So I take it that you are not coming up with me, Holmes."

"No indeed, Doctor. I still have several public houses to visit. I fear I will be quite late. I shall certainly see you in the morning, old friend."

With those words, Holmes flicked his whip and the horse clattered down the street, the hooves sharply striking the bricks in the road and echoing off the buildings.

Once inside our rooms, I settled in my chair and perused The Times. In a city the size of London, a murder on the outskirts of town was not front-page news, at least not for the staid Times. There was talk of a visit from the King of Norway and sectional troubles in Montenegro. All such foreign policy concerns dimmed when compared to a cruel murder in my eyes. It was just on eight when I heard a knock at the door and Inspector Hopkins strode into the room.

"Good evening, Doctor," he said with his hat in his hand. "I hope this call is not too late in the evening."

"Hardly that, Inspector," I replied. "Please come in and be seated."

Hopkins sat and declined an offer of a cigarette.

"Is Mr. Holmes about, Doctor?" he asked, glancing around.

"He is not," said I.

"I understand from David Highlander that Mr. Holmes has undertaken to investigate the murder of Anne Benton. Has he uncovered anything that would undercut Harold Highlander's confession?"

"I am sorry, Inspector, but even as Holmes's companion I am not in his confidences as to his thinking. When last we spoke, he was confident that he would be able to solve all questions on the morrow."

"Then his conversation with me was not mere

pique."

I remembered the crestfallen face of the young Inspector when Holmes had chastised him for his failure, as Holmes saw it, to follow up the investigation once the elder Highlander had confessed.

"Inspector, I do not believe Holmes is capable of acting from pique. The case simply does not seem complete to him. At least it did not upon hearing of the confession."

"And yet, Mr. Holmes had expected it. Why is it that Mr. Holmes cannot share his doubts and suspicions with the Yard? It is maddening, even considering the respect I have for him."

I shared the exasperation of Inspector Hopkins. At times, I too had felt the sting of my friend's refusal to share with me his inner feelings.

"Inspector, I am certain that you will hear from Holmes in the morning, if not sooner," I said, so as to soothe him.

"Where is he now, Doctor? Can you at least tell me that?"

"I can honestly say I do not know. I can only relate to you his own words. He warned me not to expect him back before the small hours, and possibly not until morning."

The Inspector was running his hands through his hair as I spoke. As I finished, he rose from his chair.

"That being the case, I will take my leave of you, Doctor," he said. "I hope to hear from Mr. Holmes, but in any event, you will likely see me tomorrow. Good evening."

The Inspector, more composed than when he had arrived, quickly exited the room and I was again left with my thoughts. I studied the notes that I had taken on the case carefully over the next few hours. Only two people had solid alibis for the time of the murder of Anne Benton. Her brother, William Benton, was far away, according to his own testimony, and could not have been on Lambs Lane, if he was being truthful. Sylvia Highlander was likewise out of the mix of suspects unless her alibi could be shaken. For the rest, opportunity was there for the taking. Neither of the Highlander men had anyone who could vouchsafe their whereabouts at the time. And even though they seemed unlikely killers, Elizabeth Woodbury and Simon Langston were virtually on the spot of the murder. Holmes had even intimated that our client, Samuel Johnson, was not above suspicion.

Once I had disposed of opportunity, I proceeded to motive. As far as I could ascertain, no motive for murder had been uncovered. The murdered lady was a relative stranger to all involved. She and her brother had been only recent transplants and they had lived, seemingly, unsullied lives. What the Inspector had said was true. Holmes had certainly expected Harold Highlander to confess, but why? It was all too baffling to me. Were it not for Holmes's doubts, I would have thought the case closed with the confession.

I realized that I was no closer to the truth than when I began, so I put away thoughts of the crime and turned to a biography of William the Conqueror. It was a weighty tome and by the time I had gotten to the Battle of Hastings, I felt my eyes grow heavy. Putting the book aside, I decided to take Holmes's advice to heart. I retired to my bed and hoped that the dawn would bring new answers.

The morning brought bright sunshine and I felt renewed energy. After performing my morning toilet, I arrived in the dining room to find that my breakfast was awaiting me, thanks to Mrs. Hudson, but that Sherlock Holmes had not returned from his odyssey. I felt sure that he would arrive in his own good time, so I decided that I would not wait breakfast. I hungrily began my meal and made short work of the larder provided.

One-half hour later, I was in the sitting room enjoying a pipe and a cup of steaming coffee, when my friend finally made his return. Instead of the livery costume that I had seen him in last, he was now dressed as a common street idler. His face was dirtied with soot and he had a bandage on one hand. He nodded silently to me and went directly to his room. I found myself eager to hear the news of his investigation, but I remained in the sitting room awaiting his return. It was not long in coming. In less than fifteen minutes my friend rejoined me and sat in his normal chair. He was once again the respectable detective that I knew well, and it was hard to believe that the creature who had passed through the room only minutes ago was the same person. Only the bandage on his hand remained from his former self. Such was the power of Holmes to conceal himself within a character. Holmes languidly packed his pipe, lit it, and leaned back in his chair with a sigh.

"I see that you have injured yourself, Holmes," said I. "How did it come about?"

"The places I have been in the last twelve hours, Doctor, are not always conducive to good health."

"Was such physical discomfort worth the information that you obtained? I take it that you were successful."

"You would be correct in that assumption, Doctor," he replied. "The case is complete. All that remains is to send a message to Hopkins and set the wheels of justice in motion."

"Do you plan to share your newfound knowledge with me, Holmes?"

Holmes looked at me and I saw a small grin play about his lips.

"You must allow me my small vanity, Watson. It is my habit to keep the cards close to the vest until the proper time, but I assure you that you will be there at the moment."

"As you will, Holmes," I said. "I know you well enough not to argue the point, but surely Hopkins will want more than your word that the case is solved."

"Of course, Doctor. I do not expect the Yard to rely upon my word alone, but there will be proof and the matter will be settled beyond all doubt. I have had answers to my cables and last night's investigation provided me with the motive for the actions that have puzzled me. The crime itself was quite simple, but I could not understand why everyone has acted as they have until last night. It cost me a gash upon my knuckles in a skirmish with a lout, but I am quite fit and it is over."

"You seem very self-satisfied I must say, Holmes."

"The case would not have been solved correctly without me, Doctor."

"That is an immodest statement, Holmes."

"False modesty is a form of self-deception, Watson. I speak only the truth."

I was considering that last statement, when the door opened and our page admitted Inspector Stanley Hopkins. Holmes waved him to a seat in an airy manner.

"You have saved me the trouble of sending for you, Inspector," said Holmes. "Your arrival is really most fortuitous."

The Inspector did not immediately reply and he had a grim expression.

"Come, Inspector, chin up," Holmes continued. "I have news that will cheer you."

"I hope so, Mr. Holmes. I could use good news."

"Why? What has happened?" asked Holmes, suddenly concerned.

"It may have nothing to do with the case, but I determined to question all concerned with the Benton murder again this morning. I sent men around to speak with everyone, but Mr. William Benton cannot be found and Mr. Simon Langston is..."

He left the statement unfinished and I felt myself leaning forward in my chair.

"Well, what of Langston?" Holmes demanded.

"He is dead, sir," replied Hopkins grimly.

CHAPTER THIRTEEN

"**D**ead," I repeated woodenly.

"Yes, Doctor," said Hopkins. "When my men knocked at his door they received no reply, so they had a look through the front window and saw him slumped in his sitting room chair. They forced the door and found he was dead."

"Do you suspect foul play, Inspector?" I asked.

"Well, he was an old man, Doctor, but under the circumstances it is odd timing at least. Of course, there is no coroner's report as yet. For that matter, we do not have the report on Miss Benton as yet, but it hardly seems necessary in her case."

"How was Mr. Langston dressed, Inspector?" asked Holmes.

"Very much as we saw him at the Benton cottage, sir. He had on trousers, shirt, jacket, and tie. Nothing out of the ordinary."

"Was the body cold upon discovery?"

"It was, sir. There has been no determination as to time of death, but it was certainly many hours before he was found."

'And do you not find that instructive?"

"What do you mean, sir?"

"Just this, Hopkins. Simon Langston was not one to stay up late. He told us that himself. Since he was fully dressed, and was cold this morning, it certainly follows that he did not die in the night, but rather the day before."

"I follow your reasoning there, sir. He died sometime yesterday before he had the chance to turn in."

"I think we can come closer than that, Inspector," said Holmes. "We can state with a certainty that he was alive up until approximately 4:30 yesterday afternoon."

"How can you be so precise, Mr. Holmes?"

"Because the good doctor had tea with the gentleman yesterday and he left him in good health, I assure you."

"You, Doctor?" Hopkins said, looking to me. "Why, whatever reason did you have to do such a thing?"

"He did so at my bidding, Inspector," said

Holmes in answer. "I asked Watson to have a cup of tea with Langston and he did so. Was the sitting-room table still set for tea at the time of the body's discovery?"

"Why, yes it was, sir."

"And were the cups filled with tea or merely the remnants?"

"I made a special note of that, sir," replied Hopkins. "Both cups were completely clean. It would appear that Mr. Langston had not yet served the tea after making it."

"That is certainly one explanation, " said Holmes vaguely. "You say that Benton has disappeared?"

"That is so, sir. He apparently left his home last evening and has not returned."

"Watson actually saw the man leaving yesterday."

"Is that so, Doctor?" asked Hopkins

I told the Inspector that it was so, and quickly related the conversation that I had had with Benton the previous day.

"That certainly tightens the timeline," said Hopkins, as he furiously scribbled in his notepad. "Now that we know it was Mr. Benton's intention to return home, his disappearance looks bad for him, I must say. I now wonder if he too has had some misfortune fall upon him."

"I think not, Hopkins," said Holmes. "I believe that you will find that Mr. Benton's disappearance and the death of Mr. Langston are not related."

"How can you be certain, Holmes?" I asked.

"Now, there you have me, Doctor," he replied. "I cannot be certain, as you say, but I believe that I can comfortably make that assumption based upon the evidence I have gathered."

"But do you believe that Simon Langston has been murdered?" challenged Inspector Hopkins.

After a short pause Holmes replied.

"I think it very likely that Mr. Simon Langston was murdered, though proving it might be beyond our means."

"Well, Harold Highlander, at least, is not a suspect," said I. "He was in gaol. A firmer alibi I cannot recall."

"That is true, Doctor. You have employed the power of deduction," said Holmes.

"Then it follows that Harold Highlander did not

murder Anne Benton," I said firmly.

"Ah, my friend, now you move from deduction to supposition," said he. "One does not necessarily follow the other."

"I suppose, Holmes, but if you are correct and Simon Langston was murdered, then we still have a killer about."

"That is so," said Holmes gravely. "I admit that I underestimated the danger. Indeed, I might have exposed you to unnecessary risk, Doctor. For that, I apologize."

"Never mind the risk to me, Holmes. What of the death of a harmless old tailor?"

Holmes made no reply. He simply relit his pipe and leaned back in his chair. Hopkins shot me a glance, but I merely shrugged my shoulders in answer. The Inspector seemed uncomfortable, but waited for Holmes to finish his pipe. Finally Holmes gave his attention to the young Inspector.

"Well, Hopkins, you seem to have something else on your mind. Out with it, man."

"You're correct, sir. I do have other news. Mr. Harold Highlander became ill during the night and a doctor was sent for. He reports that Highlander is in an advanced state of cancer. He may not live to face trial."

"Of course," said Holmes dreamily. "That again, speaks to motive."

I thought much the same, Mr. Holmes," said Hopkins. "Highlander will answer no questions on the subject of his illness, or anything else for that matter, but it defies logic to think he was not aware of his illness. With the end of his life in sight, he may have decided to settle an old score. After all, he has already been given a death sentence. Such a man has little to lose."

"Too true, Inspector," mused Holmes.

"Mr. Holmes, I confess I am not certain of what step to take next," said the Inspector. "How would you advise me to proceed?"

"Inspector, if you will be guided by me, I suggest that you bring Mr. Harold Highlander to this flat at eight o'clock tonight."

"To what end, Mr. Holmes?" Hopkins asked. "It can be done, of course, but it will certainly raise questions."

"I shall answer all questions at the appointed hour, Inspector."

"You are certain of this, Mr. Holmes?" asked the Inspector. "Is Mr. Highlander to be the only guest?"

"Certainly not," replied Holmes. "All the players of the company will be here."

"How, sir? I have no power at this time to compel their attendance."

"I will take care of the matter. Anything else?"

"Shall I continue to send inquiries looking for William Benton or will he be here as well?"

"By all means continue to energetically pursue Mr. Benton, but I think you will find that he has disappeared entirely."

"Just disappeared?" asked a skeptical Hopkins. "Surely, sir, you can tell me more than that."

"At the proper time I will, Inspector," said Holmes. "If you had made your inquiries when I advised you to, you would not be groping in the dark now."

"It is true that I had thought the case finished upon the confession of Harold Highlander," admitted the Inspector ruefully. "It is a mistake I shall not repeat, I assure you, sir."

"See that you do not, Inspector," said Holmes coldly.

With those hard words Hopkins departed, promising to return at the appointed hour. He was obviously deflated from the stern scolding from Holmes. When the Inspector's footsteps faded away, I confronted Holmes on his behavior towards his young protégé. The great man, however, blithely dismissed my concerns.

"So, you think that I have dashed his spirits, Doctor?"

"In my opinion, yes, Holmes."

"It is possible that you are right, of course, but I believe there is a time to hold a hand and a time to slap it. I judge that Hopkins will carry this memory forward with him and not repeat his error."

"It is your business, Holmes," I said. "Whom else should I expect at this evening's gathering?"

"David and Sylvia Highlander, Elizabeth Woodbury, and our client, Mr. Samuel Johnson will all be in attendance."

Holmes began writing out telegrams at his table. He finished them quickly and rang for our page. The young boy quickly answered, and scurried away with his task. Once he was gone I turned to Holmes again.

"Then, am I to understand that you were in earnest with the Inspector, and that William Benton is not expected?"

"I think it most unlikely that he will be here."

"You seem to be very blasé in your attitude towards his disappearance," said I. "Has he nothing to do with the matter we are investigating?"

"Oh, he played a role in the events, Doctor. Of that, do not doubt," said Holmes.

With those words Holmes lapsed into silence. Knowing full well the character of my friend, I did not press him further. Morning advanced into afternoon, and after our midday meal, we were relaxing over cigarettes in the sitting room when Samuel Johnson burst into the room unannounced. He was holding a telegram in one hand, and he seemed quite agitated.

"What is the meaning of this, Mr. Holmes?" he demanded, thrusting the paper towards the detective.

"The message speaks for itself, Mr. Johnson," said Holmes calmly. "Is it really that difficult to discern my intent?"

"I hired you to clear my friend and now you jape with me? I am not a man accustomed to being treated in such a manner."

"Calm yourself, Mr. Johnson, and pray be seated."

The stockbroker looked as if he wanted to argue further whilst still on his feet, but he acceded to

Holmes's request and slowly sank into a chair.

"I must apologize for my entrance," said the man, after a few moments of silence. "This entire matter has been a strain upon me, and I am not myself."

"There is no apology necessary, Mr. Johnson, I assure you," said Holmes. "The Doctor and I have seen many such entrances from clients and the authorities. Is that not so, Watson?"

I nodded my agreement to Holmes and our guest. Holmes was right, of course, that our humble rooms had seen more than one dramatic entrance. My thoughts immediately went back to our visit from Dr. Grimesby Roylott. Compared to that day, Mr. Johnson's entrance was quite sedate. I was roused from my memories by the voice of Samuel Johnson.

"I understand your need for a free hand, Mr. Holmes, but as your client, am I not entitled to some knowledge of what your thinking is on the investigation?"

"I am afraid not, sir," replied Holmes. "If the case were at a dead end I would assuredly inform you, but as it is not, you must allow my small eccentricity in presenting the solution."

"Then Harold is guiltless," said Johnson.

"I have not said that," returned Holmes.

"But your manner certainly implies..."

The stockbroker left his thought unfinished and he slumped back in his chair even further. I felt for him. His affection for Harold Highlander was palpable. I wondered if he was aware of the health of his friend, and doubted it. What would be his reaction when he discovered the dire news? Whereas Samuel Johnson had been mortified to find his friend might face prison, he would assuredly be devastated to find that Highlander was in the throes of a terminal disease.

Over the next hour, Holmes employed his most politic manner in putting off Mr. Johnson's understandable curiosity until that evening. Our client did not yield at once, but he was gradually ground down by Holmes's obstinacy in the face of his inquiries. He finally, reluctantly, departed with a promise that he would not return until the appointed hour.

Once we were alone again, Holmes began to wax eloquently to me on the subject of military deportment and dress. I had little hope that the conversation would return to more pressing matters, and I resolved to wait contentedly for eight o'clock. Still, I wondered just what the great detective had planned.

CHAPTER FOURTEEN

*B*etween seven thirty and eight o'clock our guests began to arrive. Holmes was ensconced in his bedchambers, and did not deign to make an appearance until the last chime of the clock had rung. As the final note faded, Holmes strode confidently in the room. He gave a nod to Inspector Hopkins and walked to the fireplace where he stood with his back to the assemblage. After some moments, Hopkins broke the silence of the room.

"Mr. Holmes, I have brought Mr. Harold Highlander as you asked," said the Inspector. "I have every hope that the trust I showed you in bringing him here will not be disappointed."

Holmes turned at the Inspector's words.

"Your trust will not be in vain, Inspector," he began. "I will not thank any of you for coming, as everyone is here out of self-interest, mere curiosity, or by force, as is the case with Harold Highlander."

There was a murmur of disapproval at Holmes's words, but no one assayed an out-and-out objection to them either. I looked from face to face and saw stern, worried expressions from most. David and Sylvia Highlander sat next to each other on a sofa. Elizabeth Woodbury was in my usual chair. Harold Highlander was on the settee that was normally Holmes's province, and Inspector Hopkins stood by his side. Two burly police sergeants stood guard by the door. As Holmes had prophesized, William Benton did not make an appearance.

"I was called in on this case by Inspector Hopkins because the crime seemed to be one that was out of the ordinary. A woman is beaten and stabbed in her own home. There is a note delivered to Mr. Harold Highlander that threatens her life. Mr. Highlander investigates by going to the young lady's home. Upon arrival, he is joined by Miss Elizabeth Woodbury and they discover the body. Are we all agreed so far? Mr. Highlander?

Holmes addressed the question to the elder Mr. Highlander.

"I have nothing to add to my confession, Mr. Holmes," he said stiffly. "I have already informed the Inspector that I will not play an active part in this charade. You can force my attendance, but not my participation."

The old man made a dignified presence, but if

he had hoped to stay the hand of Sherlock Holmes, he was doomed to be disappointed.

"Well, we shall see," said Holmes. "Upon my arrival at the cottage along with Dr. Watson, I immediately noticed that there were inconsistencies with the murder scene. The lady had been struck with a candlestick holder and it lay beside the body in the foyer. However, there was an oil lamp. Why would a candlestick be in that small area of the house if a lamp was there already?"

"Perhaps the lamp was empty, Mr. Holmes," said Inspector Hopkins. "That would explain it nicely."

"It would, Hopkins, if the lamp had been empty. However, I picked up the lamp. It was full of oil."

I remembered the scene as Holmes spoke. I had thought he had only casually picked up the lamp at the time. Now I saw that his mind had been keenly at work, as always.

"But what could this mean, Holmes?" I asked. "Is it important to the murder?"

"It is not a mere aside, Doctor. It is essential to understanding what happened. It means that the body was moved from its original position. And it was moved for a very important reason. It was meant to fool one very important person."

"Whom are you hinting at, Mr. Holmes?" asked Samuel Johnson.

"Let me answer you in this way," said Holmes. "Yesterday I went to the area of the murder disguised as a common livery man. In this way I was able to obtain information that was only traded between people of the same class. Much of what I learned was useless, but I came upon the one piece of information that I was looking for. This was the piece that explained Mr. Harold Highlander's actions the evening of the crime. For you see it was Mr. David Highlander who struck Miss Benton on the head with the candlestick at around four o'clock."

"What is this nonsense?" asked Sylvia Highlander. "Are you saying David struck this woman and then wrote a note so his father would read it? It makes no sense."

"It makes sense when once you factor in the fact that David Highlander and Anne Benton were having an affair. This is what I discovered last night speaking with the servants and tradesmen of the area. Inspector, you will be able to verify this now that you know what to look for. I suspect that David went to the cottage that day to break it off with Miss Benton. Or perhaps she threatened to expose him as an adulterer. Either way, he is threatened and reacts.

"Allow me to lay out the scene. David strikes the

woman and, thinking he has killed her, he leaves the cottage and returns home. He is a weak man, but not an evil one. He confesses to his father what he has done. The father leaves to go to the Benton cottage to see for himself. While the father is gone, the son drinks himself into senselessness.

"When Harold Highlander arrives on the scene, he quietly slips in the side entrance. He discovers the body of the dead girl. It was likely in the living room. He is a man of long experience and he wishes to shield his son from the grips of an unscrupulous woman. How does he do it? He decides to make it look as if the girl has been stabbed. He will then discover the body and call the authorities. But there is another problem. He must have some reason for finding the body. He comes up with the idea of the note. It is a dramatic device that gives him the motive to force the door. He makes an ample amount of noise so that Miss Woodbury is drawn out of her home. She witnesses the discovery and the police are called."

"Half a moment, Mr. Holmes," said Inspector Hopkins. "Why stab the girl and move the corpse? Why not just discover the body. The note will still serve to give him ample reason to make the discovery."

"You forget that Harold Highlander was working to deceive two separate audiences," said Holmes. "He was attempting to fool the police, to be sure, but he was also attempting to deceive his son. He was certain that when David Highlander arose from his stupor and found the girl had died from the blow to the head, that the son would confess. So he needed the son to believe that the girl had died in some other way.

"But Harold Highlander has another problem. The girl is already dead. If she is stabbed then she will not bleed. He comes up with an ingenuous idea. He will stab the girl in the chest and pour some water around the wound to make it appear wet. The only impediment to that was, that unless the Benton girl was wearing black, it would be obvious that it was water and not blood. Now, according to Mr. William Benton, the dress was part of a mourning outfit. It is highly unlikely that she was wearing it that day, so Harold Highlander quickly searched her wardrobe and found the black blouse he needed. The one that Miss Benton actually had on that day went onto the fireplace."

"So you never really believed that the shirt was used by the killer to cover up bloodstained clothing?" asked Hopkins.

"No, Inspector. I never actually advanced that theory, I merely did not disagree. No, Harold Highlander burned it because blood from the head wound must have splattered on it. There must be no question that Miss Benton was wearing the black top. At any rate, he makes the change. Once on the scene I perceived that the wet area around the wound was not blood. I clearly called attention to it."

Holmes was correct, of course. I now remembered that he had actually put his fingers into the wet area. I had not realized, nor had anyone else, the significance of his actions at the time.

"So now you see what actually happened," Holmes continued. "Mr. Harold Highlander in a bid to shield his son, moves the body into the foyer, makes it appear that the body has been stabbed, and then writes the note. He makes enough noise to ensure that another witness joins him and discovers the body. He hopes to get away with his deception, but he has already resolved to confess to the crime himself if he must. He knows he is a sick man and has already received his death warrant."

"Then I killed her," murmured David Highlander in a daze. "It all seems like a dream."

"David, say nothing," pleaded Harold Highlander. "She is already dead. You can do nothing for her."

"I can do something for my soul, Father," said a suddenly resolute David Highlander. "I should never have allowed you to take all the blame. Even if I believed your story, I at least knew it was not the whole truth. I am sorry, my dear."

Those last words were expressed to Sylvia Highlander. Her face at first was hard, but it gradually softened and she put her hand in his.

"David, you silly ass. I knew the entire time. You should have come to me. I would do anything for you."

Up until that time Sylvia Highlander had seemed a harsh woman who had little regard for her husband, but I now realized that she was desperately in love with a weak man. It had been up to her to make the difficult decisions in their family, and it had hardened her over time. But for all that, she was simply a woman in love.

"Holmes, there is something I still do not understand," said I. "What was it that caused Harold Highlander to confess to the crime? Even though you proved the note had been written at the murder scene, I thought he carried it off well. Why confess later, when it would appear he had been successful?"

"Shall I tell it, sir, or shall you?" asked Holmes.

"You are telling it well, Mr. Holmes," croaked the old man.

"It was the visit of Simon Langston," said Holmes.

"Langston?" cried Hopkins. "How was the old tailor involved?"

"Simon Langston was a bitter old man," said Holmes in reply. "He had lost his son and his investments had gone badly, but he was very crafty and astute in his own way. He had observed all that had happened that day from his sitting room."

"But he said he had been asleep during the time in question," said I.

"That is what he said, Watson, but he also talked of how he could have observed all, had he only been awake. I watched him, and he spoke directly to Harold Highlander. That was a message to Mr. Highlander that Langston knew, and wanted something for his silence. When Langston visited the Highlander estate later that same evening, he made the extortion explicit. Is that not a true account, Mr. Highlander?"

After a heavy sigh, the old man replied.

"You have said it all as it happened, Mr. Holmes. When I saw the Benton girl dead on the floor of the sitting room, I was devastated. I quickly decided that I would take my son's place. I arranged things as you said. All went as planned. The police seemed to have no case against me, and I convinced my son later that he was guiltless of murder, at least. However, Simon Langston had seen all. He openly blackmailed me that night and I resolved to confess to the crime, so as to give him no power over me or my son."

"This puts matters in a very different light," said Hopkins gravely.

"Can you not let the crime hang around my neck, Inspector," asked Harold Highlander.

"Sir, that is quite impossible," replied Hopkins.

"It is no use, Father. The truth has come out. I foolishly fell in with an evil woman," said David Highlander. He turned to Holmes. "Sir, the truth of the matter was that I went to see Anne that day to try and end the affair. She became mad with rage and flew at me with a knife. I grabbed the candlestick and struck wildly. I ran from the house like a coward and selfishly put my father in harm's way. I am ready to pay for my crime."

David Highlander stood, with some dignity and faced the Inspector. Hopkins placed a hand on his shoulder.

"You will have to come with me, sir," he intoned.

"Inspector, I ask you to wait," said Holmes.

I glanced at my friend in surprise.

"Surely the case is complete, Holmes," said I.

"Not quite, Doctor," said Holmes, "for you see, David Highlander is not guilty of murder."

CHAPTER FIFTEEN

"**M**r. Holmes, have you gone mad?" asked Inspector Hopkins in astonishment. "Are you saying that Harold Highlander did, in fact, kill Anne Benton? This is mind-boggling."

A sudden inspiration hit me.

"I think I see it, Holmes," said I.

A slight smile played across Holmes's lips.

"Shall I elucidate, Holmes?"

"By all means, Doctor."

"Very well. It occurs to me that a very deep game has been played. What if Harold Highlander did take the opportunity to murder Miss Benton? What if the first plan transpired just as you said it, Holmes? He would simply try to brazen it out and hope his position, and the confusion, would save him. Ah, but Simon Langston destroyed that plan. He could, of course, pay the blackmailer and hope to buy his silence, but that is a tricky, and dangerous, business. So he develops a fallback plan. He confesses to the crime because he knows the great Sherlock Holmes," I nodded at my friend, "will discover the inconsistencies, and will free him against his will. Or at least seemingly against his will."

"Very good, Watson," cried Holmes. "But there is an immediate flaw in the plan. How does Harold Highlander know I will continue my involvement in the case? He has confessed and Scotland Yard is satisfied."

Holmes was smiling at me as if he had successfully parried my riposte, but I had an answer.

"That is where Mr. Samuel Johnson comes in!" I said, as I dramatically pointed an accusing finger at him.

"Me?" asked the stockbroker. "Dr. Watson, I can assure you that my role in this matter is as I have described in our first meeting in this very room."

"Go on, Watson," encouraged Holmes. "You are doing wonderfully."

"As I was saying. Harold Highlander needed an ally. Someone he could trust to approach Holmes and engage him in investigating the crime, even if the authorities would not. Who is the only person he communicated with that night after Langston has made the blackmail threat? Why, it is Samuel Johnson. A man, who by his own admission, is Harold Highlander's best friend. Thus they enter into a conspiracy. As the first plan has failed, they enter into the next. Johnson hires Holmes. Holmes, as they doubtless knew he would, sees through the clumsy deception and suddenly Harold Highlander is a free man."

"What of Simon Langston, Doctor?" asked Holmes quietly. "Will he not simply make his blackmail threat again?"

"Well, there must be an answer for that," I said, with some small hesitancy.

"I should hope so, Doctor. Otherwise your scheme falls apart."

"There is one possibility, Holmes," said I. "Perhaps Simon Langston merely died. A convenient death I grant you, but you did say that one coincidence in a case is allowable. Simon Langston was an old man, and his body showed no sign of violence. Perhaps his death was a simple case of natural causes."

"Have you considered the other possibility, Doctor?" asked Holmes.

"Yes, I see what you mean," I replied.

"What other possibility?" asked Inspector Hopkins.

"Simply this, Inspector," I said, as I began to feel more confident in my role as detective. "It could be that

Harold Highlander and Samuel Johnson chose a more direct path, and Mr. Johnson murdered Simon Langston."

I heard a gasp come from one of the ladies in the room. Samuel Johnson rose to his feet in a towering rage.

"This is boldfaced slander," he said. "It is actionable, I say, and I refuse to sit here and listen further."

He made as if to leave, but Hopkins motioned towards the two sergeants by the door, and they barred his exit.

"Sit down, Mr. Johnson," said Hopkins. "We shall all see this through. Go on, Doctor."

Johnson made as if to argue the point but saw the resolute face of Inspector Hopkins and retook his seat. He sat with his arms across his chest, and his manner bespoke his anger. After a few moments of silence, Holmes spoke.

"How was Simon Langston killed, Doctor?"

"Well, as I say, Holmes, there were no signs of bodily violence, so I would imagine that some form of poison was introduced to the man."

"But does not poison generally cause unpleasant

and visible results?" Holmes asked.

"Well, yes. But it could have been any number of sleeping draughts or pain medications. An overdose of either would do the job. The victim would simply go to sleep and never wake up."

"And where would Samuel Johnson obtain such drugs, Doctor?"

"Holmes, really," I protested. "I cannot cover every contingency. I am merely suggesting a method by which the crime could have been done. In any case, Mr. Johnson could have purchased them that morning."

"But that might appear suspicious if it came to light," said Holmes, as he held up a hand to forestall another protest from me. "But for all that, I believe you have made several very able points, Doctor. Indeed, you are strikingly close to the truth in many ways."

"But there is obviously a truth that remains untold in your mind, Mr. Holmes," said Inspector Hopkins. "What is the truth? I remind you that you did gather us here to explain this riddle."

"Quite right, Inspector," said Holmes. "I shall draw this out no longer than necessary. This is what really happened to Anne Benton."

CHAPTER SIXTEEN

*T*he room was as silent as a graveyard as Holmes began to speak.

"Before I tell you who the murderer is, it is vital that you understand who Anne Benton was. The next morning after the tragedy, but before I ever spoke to Samuel Johnson, I sent off two telegrams. The first I will speak of later, but the second was to look into the background of Anne and William Benton. I was intrigued by the couple. Later that morning, I had the opportunity to meet Mr. William Benton, and my curiosity was further spurred. Watson, please describe Anne Benton."

"Well, let me see, Holmes. She was a slender woman of some thirty years. She was of medium height, very pretty, and very fair."

"Correct on all accounts. Now describe William Benton."

"He is a man, also of thirty years or so. I should think slightly older than his sister. He is a bit stout with very dark features."

"Precisely," said Holmes. "William Benton could even be described as swarthy. Do these two people thus described appear to be brother and sister?"

There was no answer, so Holmes continued.

"From what I have been able to discover through my sources, in actuality the Bentons are a husband and wife team of confidence swindlers who have changed their names countless times. They move into an area, fleece their victims, and then move on. That is why William Benton has disappeared. He could not stand any close scrutiny of his life, or the life of his so-called sister."

"But, Holmes, how could a man in the army live such a life?" I asked.

"Watson, one of the first things I learned upon meeting Mr. Benton, and one of the first things to stir my interest, was that he was not a soldier."

"How could you tell that, Mr. Holmes, just from a short meeting?" asked Inspector Hopkins.

"During that meeting, Mrs. Highlander became overcome with grief. Watson gallantly reached for his handkerchief, but Mr. Benton was quicker, and gave the lady his own. Watson, where do you keep you handkerchief?"

"Why, in my sleeve, Holmes, as you well know."

"And where was Mr. Benton's handkerchief kept?"

Before I could answer, Sylvia Highlander broke in.

"It was from his jacket pocket, Mr. Holmes. I remember distinctly. But what does that prove?"

"Only that a recently mustered out soldier would not have his handkerchief in his jacket, but rather in his sleeve. I have chided my friend Dr. Watson on more than one occasion, that he will never be taken as a true civilian as long as he maintains that practice. Now, the Highlanders have no military tradition, so they were completely taken in. Anne Benton romanced David Highlander, with a probable blackmail angle, while William Benton surveyed the area for other victims. There was one person in the area, however, who was likely not taken in by William Benton's deception. Simon Langston had a sharp eye and knew how a soldier carried himself from his son's experience. I believe that once he failed in his attempt to blackmail Harold Highlander, Langston turned his attention to other areas. Once he had taken the first step towards extortion, the next was easy. Perhaps he hinted to William Benton that he knew that his *bona fides* were not true."

"Then at that point, he murders Simon Langston

and flees," said the Inspector.

"That does not fit with the character of William Benton, Inspector. He is a man of long criminal experience, but to my knowledge he has never ventured into murder. No, Mr. Benton knows his best chance at avoiding arrest is simply to flee and begin a new identity somewhere. That is his *modus operandi*.

"So now we know the character of the murder victim. She is an unscrupulous woman who will not hesitate to use any information she discovers to her advantage. Let us imagine that she moves into the cottage and gives a sympathetic ear to a neighbor who is in some distress. That neighbor's father has recently passed away. He was in much pain towards the end and the neighbor confesses that she aided his death with an overdose of morphine. Such a woman might bleed said neighbor dry. Does this sound familiar to you, Miss Woodbury?"

All eyes turned to Elizabeth Woodbury. She faced Holmes, and I saw anger in her eyes. She was still heavily powdered, so it was impossible to tell if her cheeks were flushed.

"You go too far, Mr. Holmes," she said evenly. "You openly accuse me of the murder of my father and the death of Miss Benton? I suppose next you will say that I murdered Simon Langston, as well."

"That is exactly what I was going to say next, my dear. However, I believe that the death of your father was a mercy killing. It is common knowledge that he was terminal. Even the death of Anne Benton is somewhat understandable. She has tormented you and drained your resources. Those same resources that you had hoped to use to continue your travels. You saw an opportunity and you struck. It was not an action of cold blood, but a reflex against an evil woman. The death of Simon Langston is harder to forgive, but every murder makes the next one less difficult."

"You can prove nothing against me, sir," said the lady.

"We shall see," said Holmes. "Here is what actually happened that evening from your point of view. You see David Highlander flee from the house in agitation. Your curiosity is aroused. You go over through the side door of the cottage facing your own house, which was open. You find Anne Benton bloodied on the floor. You think for a minute that she is dead. You are free, you think, but upon closer inspection you discover that she is merely unconscious. She should be dead, she must be dead. You begin to strangle her, but she awakens and fights back. However, she is in a weakened condition and you prevail."

"Strangulation?" said Hopkins. "This is the first I am hearing of it."

"Had you examined the body more closely, you would have noticed what I did," said Holmes. "The eyes of the victim were shot through with blood. This is a common symptom of strangulation and certainly not of stabbing or bludgeoning."

"Of course," I muttered. I recalled Holmes pulling back the eyelids and seeing the bloodshot eyes.

"I cannot believe that I missed that, Mr. Holmes," said the Inspector glumly.

"Do not take it too badly, Hopkins," said Holmes. "The scene that was presented was a powerful one. It was designed to make onlookers believe that the murder happened a certain way. It was a compelling misdirection. Now where was I? Oh yes, Miss Woodbury, once the murder is done, you leave by the same way you entered and are careful to rake the ground surrounding the small patio to cover your footprints, but to leave the footprint of David Highlander, so as to incriminate him. This is the print Harold Highlander nearly obliterates later."

"How are you certain of that, Holmes?" I asked.

"Because the gardener had not been at the work for several days, yet the rake was leaning against the house next to the door. There were also only the two sets footprints of Harold Highlander and Miss Woodbury in the sand later, and the single print of David

Highlander. Surely there would have been other prints if she had not smoothed the area. In any case, she awaits the discovery of the body. She has likely decided to tell the police that she saw David Highlander fleeing the scene, hoping for his arrest. However, her plans are upset by Harold Highlander. When she enters the room with him, she is prepared to pretend to be shocked by the death of her neighbor, but she finds herself genuinely surprised at the murder scene Harold Highlander has constructed, and the tale of the note that he says he received. She wisely decides to remain silent and await developments. She must have been thrilled when, to her surprise, Harold Highlander confessed.

"There is however, one last loose end, Miss Woodbury. You must also have realized the import of Simon Langston's words that night in the cottage when he spoke of how he would have seen all, if only he had been awake. He was trying to send a message to Mr. Highlander, but it must have chilled your bones, as well. I believe that yesterday you visited Mr. Langston for tea. At the first opportunity you drugged his beverage and caused his death in the same manner that you had done with your father. All those who can injure you are now dead, and you can relax for the first time in an age. That is, if you can live with your conscience."

"That is a very pretty tale, Mr. Holmes," Miss Woodbury replied, "but a tale with little evidence that I can see."

"It is true that your involvement in the death of your father and of Mr. Langston will be difficult to prove, but I believe that I can demonstrate that you strangled Anne Benton," said Holmes evenly.

"How, Mr. Holmes?" asked Inspector Hopkins. "I believe that you have accurately described what has occurred, but as the lady says, much of it is supposition. Can you even prove the ongoing blackmail of Miss Woodbury by Miss Benton?"

"Only by following a logical train of facts. Miss Woodbury stated that her father left her very little, to her surprise, she said. However, Samuel Johnson, who was stockbroker for Miss Woodbury's father, states he left her a tidy sum. One of these statements is incorrect. One of the wires I sent out the day after the murder was an inquiry into Miss Woodbury's finances. I am told that they have been steadily drained since a date that is curiously close to the date on which the Bentons became her neighbors. If the bank account of Anne Benton shows deposits that match those withdrawals, then we can establish motive."

"But what of the murder itself, Holmes?" I asked. "Even if the coroner's report states that strangulation is the cause of death, how can you tie Miss Woodbury to it?"

In answer, Holmes turned to the Inspector.

"Hopkins, in your experience, how does a person react to being strangled?"

"It has been my observation that they flail at their attacker, Mr. Holmes."

"It is my observation as well," said Holmes. "With that in mind, I closely examined the fingernails of the victim. The nails were clean and finely shaped, though very short. You observed it as well, I think, Doctor."

"It is as you say, Holmes. It seemed distinctly unstylish for such a beautiful woman, I remember thinking."

"I deduced from the length of the nails of the victim that she had scratched her assailant and that there had been tissue under her nails from this. The killer realized her dilemma at once and took steps so that no one would ever associate scratches with the crime. She cut the nails short and shaped them as only another woman could. With that evidence gone, even if someone suspected strangulation, they would not be on the lookout for someone who displayed scratches."

Suddenly it occurred to me what Holmes was driving at. I looked over at Elizabeth Woodbury and noted again how heavily powdered her face was.

"Miss Woodbury, if we were to remove your

make-up would we find fresh scratch marks beneath it?" asked Holmes.

The lady sat for some time, saying nothing. She had her hands folded primly on her lap with her eyes down. She finally lifted her chin and met the gaze of Sherlock Holmes.

"It proves nothing, Mr. Holmes," she said with authority. "I merely scratched my face on a rose bush while gardening. It is vanity to hide it, of course, but it means nothing."

"That is well parried, Miss Woodbury, but the scratches you are hiding along with the evidence of the blackmail payments will surely be enough to convict you of murder. Besides, now that the police know to look for morphine as a cause of death for Simon Langston, I am confident that they will find it. I remind you that you told of your access to morphine when you related the story of your father's death."

"I have heard enough," said Inspector Hopkins. He took the lady by the arm. "Miss Woodbury, I must ask you to accompany me to Scotland Yard."

"Of course, Inspector," she said. She stood in a dignified manner.

As the Inspector was walking her to the door, they passed closely by Holmes. The lady paused and spoke softly to him.

"I loved my father a great deal, Mr. Holmes. For some reason, it is very important to me that you believe that."

"Why, I do, my dear, I assure you," he replied graciously.

CHAPTER SEVENTEEN

*A*fter the room had cleared, Holmes resumed his customary chair and lit a pipe. We sat in silence for some minutes. Holmes had come through again where the authorities had failed, but there were still some lingering questions in my mind.

"I say, Holmes," I began, "you made it sound as if you suspected Miss Woodbury from the start. Is that so?"

"Quite so, Watson. I saw at once that the murdered woman had been strangled, and when I saw the nails of Anne Benton and the heavy powdered make-up on Miss Woodbury I felt sure that I had identified the culprit."

"But why not accuse her at that point? You could have solved the case that night."

"It is true that I could have determined that Miss Woodbury had murdered Miss Benton, but that would not have explained why she did. I also wanted to know why Harold Highlander rearranged the murder scene to disguise the culprit. At first I thought it possible that they were in the murder together, but, of course, I later realized that the father was covering for the son. I have an orderly mind, Doctor, and I prefer an orderly solution. I believe that answers your question."

"It does, Holmes," I replied. "But you must realize that your orderly process came at a cost."

"What cost would that be, Doctor?"

"Why, the death of Simon Langston," I cried.

"Ah, yes. Very unfortunate," said Holmes blandly.

"I must say, Holmes, that you do not express much regret for the death of the old tailor."

"Why should I feel regret?"

"Holmes, this is a callous attitude. Have you no feeling for your fellow man?"

"Doctor, this a wearying conversation. Simon Langston, however spotless his life was up until that point, was engaged in the blackmail of not just one, but two, and possibly three people. He certainly extorted Harold Highlander, I believe he did so with Miss Woodbury as well, and I believe that his next target was William Benton. In addition, he gave false evidence to the authorities and helped to cover up a murder. Does this sound like the life of a good and moral man?"

"I see your point, Holmes, but the sentence for blackmail is not death."

"That is very true, of course, Doctor, but Simon Langston was playing a very dangerous game and he has paid. Recall what happens to those who sow the wind."

"They reap the whirlwind," I murmured. Holmes had a point, of course. Langston had engineered the events that led to his death, yet I still felt for the lonely old man. How many nights, I wondered, had he nursed the memory of his son's death until it blackened his soul? I had an involuntary shiver at the thought of creeping evil.

"You seem very pensive, Doctor," said Holmes. "I take it that you find my arguments unpersuasive as to Langston."

"It is done, Holmes, and I am certain you did as your own conscience dictated. However, there is still one mystery that remains unanswered."

"And what would that be?"

"Why, the teapots, Holmes. Do not tell me that you have forgotten them."

"Indeed not, Watson, but I do not see the question."

"There are two questions actually," said I. "What was the importance of the teapots, and why did Sylvia Highlander destroy Miss Woodbury's pot? It seemed very incriminating to me."

"I confess, Watson, that the teapots were a mere device so as to give you a reason for your visit."

"A reason you kept hidden from me, I take it."

"Regretfully, yes, Doctor," said Holmes. "Please do not take offense. I am afraid that you are quite incapable of guile." I made as if to dispute him, but he stayed my hand. "It is only because duplicity is at war with your good and honest nature. It is not a reflection upon your intelligence, I assure you."

I was somewhat mollified by that explanation.

"What I actually sent you to see that day was whether Langston was expecting a visitor, and you performed that job admirably."

"I made no such report, one way or the other, Holmes," I protested.

"But you did, Doctor. You told me that there were two teacups out that day. Langston was not a man with friends to stop by. He told us himself that he was alone in the world. What those two cups told me was that he expected a guest. That guest, I was sure, was

Miss Woodbury. You confirmed that with your visit to her cottage."

"How? The only thing of note I can recall is that Sylvia Highlander broke the teapot."

"Then you do not recall all. You reported that Mrs. Highlander told you that she had insisted Miss Woodbury brew a pot of tea."

I gave Holmes a look of bewilderment.

"Don't you see, my friend? She had not made tea because she was going to Langston's cottage for tea. He had thought she was coming to find out his demands for silence; however, she had other plans."

"I still find it hard to believe that she killed the old man in cold blood."

"Two days earlier she would not have imagined it herself, but she was a trapped animal. And as I said, once you commit the first murder, the second comes all too easily."

"But then why did Sylvia Highlander shatter the pot?"

"That is the one coincidence we allowed for, Doctor. It did come at an odd time from your point of view, but pots do break."

I gave no answer to that, as there was no answer to give. Holmes let a smile play about his lips and seemed content with my discomfort. I resolved to give Holmes no further opportunity to have sport with me that night, and I reached for a book. At that moment the door to our rooms opened, and Mycroft Holmes strode in.

"Why, Mycroft, what a pleasant surprise," said Holmes. "You have saved me a trip to the Diogenes Club. Please, be seated."

Mycroft lowered his bulk into an armchair. I was shocked to see the portly man. He rarely left his usual haunts. I wondered what must have brought him.

"How are things with you, Sherlock?" he asked politely.

"I am well. You have just missed the resolution of the Benton murder case."

"It was the neighbor, Miss Woodbury, of course," said Mycroft.

"Naturally," said Holmes.

"I thought as much. It seemed obvious from the newspaper accounts I read."

"Is that what has brought you here? Did you fear that I would make a misstep? At any rate, I am pleased that you are here. What news is there on the Masterson case? Was the booty on *The Gadfly* as we surmised?"

Mycroft Holmes shifted uncomfortably in his chair.

"That is why I am here, Sherlock," he said. "For you see, I am afraid I let the matter slip from my mind. By the time I recalled it and notified the ministry, *The Gadfly* had already disembarked from Aberdeen."

"This is grave news, Mycroft," cried Holmes. "Once the ship reaches America, all will be lost."

"The port master says the ship was bound for New York."

"But, of course, you realize that they will actually sail for New Orleans," stated Holmes.

"Of course," agreed Mycroft, nodding his head sagely. "I will report to the ministry this new development, and take care of the details."

"That will not be necessary," said Holmes. "I will send the appropriate telegrams this very night. The noose will tighten around Masterson's neck yet."

"I do feel as though I have let you down, Sherlock," said Mycroft. "I cannot imagine how I let the matter slip from my mind."

"Do not give it another thought," said Holmes. "Is there anything else on your mind? You appear troubled?"

"I have heard of a murder on Montague Street. It seemed quite odd."

"What was it that was so odd?"

"Well, Sherlock, the man was murdered in your old rooms."

"Tell me all that you know," said Holmes, leaning forward eagerly.

The End

SPECIAL NOTE

If you've read and enjoyed The Sherlock Holmes Uncovered Tales, please add a review at the site on which you purchased your copy. Reviews provide a valuable guide for those attempting to find books they might enjoy.

Thank you,

Steven Ehrman

The Lambs Lane Affair

Steven Ehrman

Made in the USA
Middletown, DE
04 October 2016